THE THINNING VEIL
13 TWISTED TALES

By

Matthew J. Pallamary

Mystic Ink Publishing

Mystic Ink Publishing
San Diego, CA
www.mysticinkpublishing.com

ISBN 10: 0-9986809-9-0 (sc)
ISBN 13: 978-0-9986809-9-6 (sc)

Library of Congress Control Number: 2023907565
Mystic Ink Publishing, San Diego, CA

Book Jacket and Page Design: Matthew J. Pallamary / San Diego CA
Cover artwork: Alfredo Zagaceta C / Pucallpa Peru
Author's Photograph: Matthew J. Pallamary — Robert DeLaurentis / Santa Barbara CA

Dedication

You asked for more fiction, so this book is dedicated to you, Alice Rondeau Hinchliffe. Thank you for all the encouragement and support you have given me over the years from my very first scribbles to all the manuscripts you read during the course of my evolution as a writer. This extends by proxy to your hubby Terry, one of the best bros anybody could ever ask for.

TABLE OF CONTENTS

INTRODUCTION

Art imitates life and reflects our human condition which fluctuates from moment to moment along with our ever-changing life experience of the times we live in.

My first short story collection, ***The Small Dark Room of the Soul and Other Stories*** was published thirty years ago and made references to the collective fears of those times. Much has happened over the last three decades since then with shifting geopolitics, explosive growth in science, technology, pandemics, school shootings, chaotic weather patterns, homelessness, and all the other problems we are still struggling with as we move deeper into the twenty-first century.

Though some of the cultural references are dated in light of current and recent events, the message is just as relevant now as it was then, maybe even more so, so I am repeating the introduction to ***The Small Dark Room of the Soul and Other Stories*** here.

There can be no light without darkness.

The sun cannot rise without the night preceding it, and the setting sun of the day must inevitably fade to black. If life were all sunshine and roses, there would be no contrast. Perpetual sunshine would be both blinding and devastating. We need the darkness. It is an integral part of the whole.

Part of us.

Horror stories are a reflection of our darker side. In an age of very real terrors like A.I.D.S., cancer, and terrorism, stories that frighten us can perform a useful function by allowing readers to live out and experience fear in a controlled fashion and deal with horror on their own terms. If it gets to be too much, they can always close the book and put it away. Experiencing horror in this way works as an anxiety release because it is a tangible way to deal with and escape the terrors of modern living.

The emotion of horror keeps us in touch with the darker aspects of ourselves while allowing us to confront our own vulnerability and inevitable death. Reading horror is a valve that allows steam to escape when the buildup is too great, yet the fictionality of it gives us an escape from a confrontation that could overwhelm us. It provides a cathartic release without oppressing us with more than we can handle.

Too often we shun our dark side in hopes that if we don't see it, it doesn't exist. Yet give us an Ed Gein, Charlie Manson, Ted Bundy, Hannibal Lecter, Jeffrey Dahmer, or any other grisly example of the dark side of human nature, and we express a morbid fascination that borders on frenzy.

We can't help but slow down on the highway to gawk at the carnage of another's untimely, messy death or sneak that guilty peek at another's deformity or misfortune.

We just have to look.

How many Jeffrey Dahmer jokes have we laughed at, then in the same breath said how disgusting it all is.

Strange creatures, human beings.

Fact is, our dark side is an inescapable part of our makeup. There's a little bit of Hannibal and Jeffrey in all of us, the problem is most of us don't want to acknowledge it.

Through the ages, countless spiritual disciplines have urged us to look within ourselves and seek the truth. Part of that truth resides in a small, dark room -- one we are afraid to enter. If we can only push aside the dark door of fear that holds us at bay and rescue the part of our souls that cringes in the dark, we might come to a better understanding of what makes us tick.

We have to take this unmentionable part of ourselves out into the light of truth so we can know its nature, because if we are to confront the uncomfortable truth, we must look in the face of the demon and admit that it is in us. When we're finished, we can let the monster crawl back into its dark abyss until the next play time.

If you're timid of spirit and afraid of the dark, it's time to take a look at what lies behind your own door of fear so you can glimpse the twisted evil that lies in *all* of us. Within these pages we can play with it, poke it, and probe it in hopes that we may better understand the wholeness that makes up our being.

Who says we can't have fun doing it? After all, the little monster *is*

part of us.
    March 1994   **M.P.**

Twenty years later, my second short story collection, **A Short Walk to the Other Side** was published, following the similar theme of how close we all are to our demons, no matter how much we try to ignore and rid ourselves of them. We are all just a short walk away from a thought, act, or emotion that lets the monster out of its cage, taking us hostage into the abyss with it, sometimes with no escape.

The introduction to this second collection, **A Short Walk to the Other Side** follows.

Who are we really?

What or where are the boundaries between what we believe to be real and what we imagine?

Ancient tribal cultures gave equal credence to dreams, visions, and their waking worlds, treating them all as different degrees of one and the same all-encompassing reality.

Do we in fact know ourselves or our *true* nature?

How many times have we reacted impulsively, only to regret our actions later, often with the apology, "I'm sorry, I'm not myself today," or "I don't know what got into me."

In these moments of intense feeling, if we are not ourselves, then who or what are we?

Where do we *really* live?

The fact that the question arises makes the "other" implicit within ourselves. What is this "other"? Duality? Plurality? Divided self? Are we possessed by something other than ourselves or are we in denial of our other selves because we find their behavior unacceptable?

Do we possess them or do they possess us?

This quandary became the theme of an old time radio show that started with: "Who knows what lurks in the hearts of men? The Shadow knows."

How well do we know our shadows as individuals and collectively? Better still, how well do our shadows know us?

Regardless of who is "running the show" at any point in space and time, every choice we make can change our life forever, along with the lives and destinies of others. A momentary lapse of attention while driving can cripple, maim, or bring swift and sudden death.

One moment of careless passion can leave you responsible for another life or bring the imminent end of your own from any number of ghastly diseases. A brief moment of passionate anger can land you in prison for the rest of your time on this earthly plane.

What doors do we pass through when we choose and what are the consequences of our actions? Better still, where do they leave us?

Coincidences, synergistic moments, timing, attitude, emotion, and attention can all change in the span of a single breath. What really goes on in the human heart and mind?

We cringe when we hear of, or witness heinous behavior and inhuman cruelty, yet human beings murder each other with endless and ingenious weapons of death, often in the name of a higher power.

Such disregard for life is difficult to comprehend, yet humans kill each other more than any other species. We are all human, so all of us are capable of making that one life altering choice that brings us someplace alien and unexpected.

Most people stay deeply entrenched in the cultural mainstream. Feeling safe and sane in their routines, they avoid those living on the fringes, believing that they could never sink so low and never think or act in such odd and terrifying ways, but we are all human, living within the same realm of possibilities. We all have our shadow selves. How much does it take to send us over the edge?

The truth is that it is a lot shorter walk to the other side than we like to think.

This, my third short story collection, **_The Thinning Veil_** follows the same train of thought. In this case it doesn't matter if the demons are locked in a small dark room, or just a short walk away, because the veil between the worlds is thinning and the boundaries have become blurred, bringing more weight to the question; what or where are the boundaries between what we believe to be real and what we imagine?

NOT FROM HERE

His eyes flickered open after a gentle kick in his side, making him squint at the bright sunlight. He saw the foot and followed the leg up to see two people dressed in blue with shiny metal on their chests leaning over him.

"Hey Ace," the taller one with short hair said in a deep baritone. "What do you think you are doing lying around in the middle of Central Park in your birthday suit?"

"Where are your clothes?" the short one with long hair, bigger breasts, and a higher pitched voice asked.

He looked as puzzled as they did as to how he came to be naked and exposed in the warm sunlight and appeared to struggle trying to articulate an answer but he said nothing.

"OK pal," the bigger one said with a hint of aggression in his voice. "Let's see some identification."

He looked around bewildered.

"Do you think he was robbed?" The smaller one leaned in closer and looked into his eyes. "Are you all right? Where are your clothes, your I.D.? Are you hurt? Have you been assaulted or robbed?"

No response came.

"We can't have you lying around here like this," the bigger one said. "It's against the law. You have no clothes, no I.D. and no excuses."

The woman cop frowned. "Do you think he might be deaf, mute, or both?"

Her partner shook his head. "He ain't deaf, Marie. I can tell by his facial expressions that he hears what we're saying and he's reacting to us. Maybe he's high on something."

"Or maybe he's mute."

"There's no way of telling without him saying anything. He doesn't appear to be a threat to anyone, but we can't leave him here in the middle of the park naked as a jaybird."

"Sorry to spoil your day," the woman said, "but my partner is right. You have no identification and no answers to our questions, and you have no clothes on, so we have no choice but to take you in. We can't leave you here like this. Besides, you'll get sunburned lying here exposed the way you are and someone who is not so friendly could hurt you."

The bigger one leaned in and said a little louder. "Do you have family or someone we can contact?"

He looked from one to the other with a blank expression, then the two cops looked at each other and the woman shrugged.

"Go get a blanket from the squad car so we can cover him up and get him out of here without a lot of fuss," the bigger cop said. "I'll stay here and keep an eye on him."

The woman gave him a quick nod and walked away while the man grabbed a microphone from his shoulder. "Dispatch, this is unit twelve in Central Park. We have a naked male in his mid to late thirties about six feet tall with long brown hair, a beard, and blue eyes that we are taking into custody. He looks clean, fit, well groomed, and appears nonviolent and fully conscious. He seems to hear what we say, but is unresponsive to our questions."

"Copy that," a staticky voice responded.

He pulled a cell phone from his pocket and took a picture. "I'm texting you a picture and need you to check missing persons, Bellevue, and other hospitals as well as any mental health facilities, immigration, or other possible sources where he might have come from."

"Ten four," dispatch responded.

"We have a twenty minute ETA to the precinct and will check in when we get there to see what you come up with."

"Ten four."

The woman returned with an olive green blanket and her partner extended his hand to the man who reached out and took it.

"No need to cuff him," the male cop said. "Aside from being uncommunicative and in his birthday suit, he isn't putting up any resistance and he hasn't done anything threatening. We don't want to traumatize him, especially if he's come from a treatment center of some kind."

"Copy that, Joe." The woman took his other hand and they pulled him into an upright sitting position. She draped the blanket over his shoulders, then leaned in close and studied him a moment. "I don't think he's on anything. He has the clearest most serene eyes I've ever seen – and he looks and smells so clean!"

"Unlike the other funky homeless people we usually have to deal with."

They helped him to his feet and walked to the squad car with him in between them. He stayed docile and cooperative while they helped him into the back seat behind the caged partition.

The woman drove while he looked out at the passing scenery with childlike wonder from the back seat.

The male cop looked in the rear view mirror, his eyes meeting the blue-eyed innocence of their passenger. "Aside from your lack of clothes and identification you don't strike me as being mentally challenged or impaired. Are you sure you don't want to tell us where you came from, or have any family members or anyone else we can notify to get you sorted out?"

"We're not going to hurt you and only want what is best for you," the woman added, glancing at him in the mirror.

His eyes and facial expression seemed to acknowledge her, but he remained mute.

The squad car's radio crackled with the dispatcher's voice, "A gang fight in progress on one hundred eleventh street and Park Ave. All available units check in and respond."

The two cops looked at each other while unit after unit checked in and reported heading to the crime scene, then the driver said, "unit twelve enroute ETA 5 minutes."

Their passenger's eyes grew wide and his mouth dropped when the siren came on accompanied by flashing blue lights.

A few moments later the dispatcher spoke again. "Unit twelve, we have a strong turnout of first responders and you have a civilian in transport, so remain in a backup position when you arrive at the scene to minimize any danger to your passenger."

"Ten four."

Two minutes later the siren stopped and they pulled up into a sea of flashing blue lights behind a group of squad cars that gave them a full view of a street brawl between biker gangs becoming more contained as cops in riot gear, batons, and shields advanced on it.

Fists flew, knives flashed, while baseball bats and chains swung. Blood spattered and some fell while others hobbled, but most fought with savage intensity.

"I'm not from here!" the man in the back seat blurted.

The two cops looked at each other astonished, then turned their attention to the back seat to see their once serene passenger pale-skinned and wide-eyed with fear, shaking his head no.

"What did you say?" the male cop asked.

"I'm not from here!"

"If you aren't from here, then where are you from?"

He continued shaking his head no. "I'm not from here."

Outside, the other cops had broken up the fight. Uniforms and paramedics swarmed in and a stream of injured and arrested were carted off to ambulances, paddy wagons, and squad cars.

"Where *are* you from?" The woman asked in a gentler tone.

He continued shaking his head no and said nothing more.

The radio crackled. "The situation is under control and no further assistance is needed. Unit twelve proceed with your transport."

The driver looked to her partner and shrugged, then backed the squad car away from the scene. Their passenger crew calm again as the sea of flashing blue lights receded behind them.

"As I said before We're here to help you," she said. "There's no need to be afraid."

"Now that we know you can talk," the man said, "tell us who we can contact so we can get you squared away."

"I'm not from here," their passenger said, matter-of-factly.

The male cop studied him in the rear view mirror and saw him looking out at the passing scenery with the same childlike wonder he had before.

"He ain't cooperating," the cop said, "but I don't think he's bullshitting us either. I don't think he's playing with a full deck."

"We'll get him ID'd once we're back at the precinct," the driver said. "Without any ID there's no way of running a background check so we don't know if he has any priors or anything else for that matter, but I'm betting he's clean by the way he's been acting."

"Copy that. Once we check his prints, if we don't find anything local I'm thinking that the INS and Homeland Security will have some records. If he is an illegal, he might not know any English."

"That would explain his limited vocabulary."

Other than the occasional crackle from the radio and the dispatcher's voice they rode the rest of the way to the precinct in silence.

"He really does seem to be an innocent," the woman said when they pulled into the lot, "but we'd better cuff him when we bring him in. After that last little panic let's be gentle."

She pulled into a parking space and her partner stepped out, opened the back door and extended his hand to help the man out. "Take it easy, Ace," he said. "No one's going to hurt you."

He looked up with a childlike gaze and let the bigger cop help him out without resisting, leaving the blanket behind. He didn't react when the woman guided his hands behind his back and slipped the cuffs on, then she reached into the car, grabbed the blanket and draped it over his shoulders, wrapping it around him and securing it with a Tie Wrap like a cloak. Putting him between them, the two cops guided him into the station without incident.

He looked around as if seeing everything for the first time while plainclothes and uniforms moved about in a flurry of activity. They made their way to a middle-aged man with curly graying hair behind a countertop at the back of the room sitting at a computer terminal. His nametag said MORASH. CNN showed the news on a big flat screen television behind a glass enclosed waiting area off to one side.

"Hey Jack," the woman said, leaning on the counter.

"Hey Joe, Marie." Morash looked up from his terminal and nodded toward their long haired bearded charge whose serene blue eyes, guileless expression, and well-groomed appearance combined with the blanket draped over him like a cloak made him look Christlike. "I ran your suspect's picture through some databases and came up empty."

Joe sighed. "Shit! We can't process him without knowing who he is."

Marie shook her head. "Another John Doe."

"More like Jesus Doe if you ask me," the man behind the counter said. "Better get his prints so we can look him up in that database."

Jack put a fingerprint scanning device that connected to his computer up on the counter.

"We're going to print you so we can find out who you are and help you get settled," Marie said, removing his cuffs.

His arms dangled at his sides and he showed no reaction when Marie pressed his fingers onto the scanner, then he became fascinated with the device and the process when the LEDs flashed, registering each print. He stared at his hands with a puzzled expression when they finished as if discovering them for the first time. Joe and Marie exchanged glances, then looked at Jack behind the counter who shrugged.

"I'll run these through some more databases," Jack said, "and we'll

17

see what turns up so we can figure out where he belongs. Shouldn't take long."

"OK Ace." Joe put his hand on their prisoner's shoulder, stirring him from his stupor and guided him away from the counter.

Jesus Doe looked into Joe's eyes with the trusting innocence of a three year old until a muffled booming sound from the big flat screen behind the glass enclosed waiting area caught his attention. His eyes grew wide at the sights and sounds of guns and explosions from a war being reported on CNN.

"I'm not from here!" he shrieked staggering backward.

He flailed when Joe grabbed for him, sending them both tumbling to the floor. Uniforms swarmed in to assist, pinning him to the floor while Marie snapped the cuffs back on, then they pulled him to his feet.

"I'm not from here," he said in a half-whisper between sobs while staring at the ground shaking his head no like a petulant child.

"We better keep him out of the general population until we get him sorted out," she said.

"Good idea." Joe brushed himself off and straightened his uniform. "I don't think he'd stand much of a chance being thrown in with all those lowlifes."

Jesus Doe didn't resist when they hustled him to an interrogation room with a steel door and a small window where they locked him in.

"We sure got us a live one this time," Marie said as they walked back to the booking counter."

Joe shook his head. "In all my years on the force, I've never seen anything like this. He never tried to hit me or make any aggressive moves toward me. He was just scared shitless and wanted to get away."

"Let's see what Jack came up with so we can move this along and get on with more important duties."

They found Jack back at the booking desk frowning at his monitor.

"What's the deal?" Joe said.

Jack held out his hands. "So far no record of him."

"What?"

"I searched our database here in the city, then hospitals, institutions, and jails statewide. Because you found him in his birthday suit, for shits and giggles I also checked morgues and funeral homes. No priors, and for that matter no record of him at all. I'm now rerunning his prints and pictures through state databases. I'm thinking that he must be an illegal alien, so I'm querying Homeland Security, the N.S.A., D.O.J., I.N.S., F.B.I., C.I.A., D.E.A., and the Federal

Bureau of Prisons. I'm also asking them to expedite and extend their searches to Interpol and other foreign agencies. It's going to take a while, so why don't you guys go back out on patrol. I'll have dispatch contact you when we come up with something."

"Wow!" Marie said. "We sure picked a doozy this time."

"No shit," Joe said. "Thanks Jack. We'll be waiting to hear from you to find out who the *real* Jesus Doe is."

Jack gave a wry smile and winked. "Don't worry, we'll find him."

Marie winked back. "My money's on you, Jack."

Two hours later the call came in from dispatch. "Unit 12, report to the precinct booking desk immediately. What's you twenty?"

Joe grabbed the mike. "Unit twelve reporting in. We're at Central Park West."

"What's your ETA?"

"Fifteen minutes."

"Get here as soon as you can."

"Ten four."

Joe looked at Marie who was frowning. "I hope our Jesus Doe is alright."

She nodded. "I have to admit, that as weird as he is, I have a little soft spot for him. Aside from his little freak outs, he was pretty harmless."

"Like an innocent little kid."

"Exactly."

They pulled into the precinct lot and hurried to the booking desk where they found Jack waiting for them looking apprehensive.

"What gives?" Joe said. "Is Jesus Doe alright?"

Jack shook his head. "I ran every search imaginable and came up empty on all counts, including everything from any foreign agencies. There's no record of anything, no birth, no immigration records. Nada." He kept shaking his head. "It's as if he never existed."

"Are you shitting me?" Marie said.

"I wish I was. The feds have stepped in and two NSA investigators are on their…" Jack pointed to two men in black suits with military style haircuts approaching the desk with precinct ID's on their jackets. "That must be them."

"It's the men in black!" Marie said.

"Maybe they Neuralized Jesus Doe," Jack quipped.

Joe chuckled. "That would explain his lack of vocabulary."

The two nearly identical looking agents marched up to the desk and flashed badges. One of them looked a little older than the other. "Agents McKendry and Collins, NSA," he said with authority. "We're here to take your John Doe into custody."

Joe snorted. "You mean Jesus Doe. Good luck with that!"

"What do you mean by that?" the agent said, sounding both authoritative and irritated.

"You'll see," Marie said. "Come on."

They led the two agents to the interrogation room where Joe unlocked the door. "He's all yours."

The two agents pushed past him and stopped in the doorway.

"What the hell is going on here?" the older one demanded. "Heads are going to roll for this little stunt!"

Joe went in first. "What the fu…"

Marie stepped in behind him and stared dumbfounded at the blanket piled in the corner of the vacant room and the handcuffs on the floor beside it.

THE CINDERELLA SYNDROME

A group of students, researchers, and journalists in a darkened laboratory in Boston watched a clump of human brain cells light up in flashes of activity onscreen as they settled into a living mouse brain on a computer monitor next to a microscope.

Towering over his audience, lanky, dark-haired Justin Perez PhD looked up from the monitor and addressed the group. "These cells are sprouting new connections a few centimeters long that are forming networks with each other." He smiled. "It's all they want to do and I can't tear them away."

"It's a mad love affair," Rebecca, his short, stocky red-haired assistant said. Her pixie cut, freckles, thick glasses, and plump face looked childlike, as if she were playing dress up in her white lab coat.

"Aren't you concerned about creating some kind of hybrid monster?" a petite blonde-haired student with innocent blue eyes asked.

Perez stood up straighter. "We're one of just a handful of labs able to study human neural cells at work in a live, developing brain, something that is typically off limits for ethical and technical reasons. We can't study these processes as they unfold in a fetal human brain, so we watch human cortical neurons mature and form active networks in a live animal. Our research focuses on a specialized type of neural chimera that allows us to manipulate live human neurons."

Our work has already yielded important insights into health and disease," Rebecca added.

"What kind of insights?" the blonde asked.

"Using neural chimeras we have found differences in how neurons develop and behave in Down's syndrome and Alzheimer's disease."

21

A heavy-set man with short black curly hair and thick glasses wearing a press pass cleared his throat. "I read an article that accused researchers of playing God, and there have been warnings about blurring the lines between humans and other animals, or the possibility of creating human-like perception and cognition in one of these hybrids. Is this really a good model for answering a scientific question or are we pushing boundaries for the sake of it? At what point would a collection of human neurons in another animal's brain become something that deserves a unique moral status?"

Rebecca opened her mouth to respond, but Perez held up his hand and his smile thinned into a hard line. "Playing God!" He snorted and shook his head. "The US National Academies of Science, Engineering, and Medicine have encouraged pilot studies like ours and they oversee close monitoring of animals to identify any new or unusual behaviors. We have the honor of being one of those pilot studies."

"So the government keeps a close eye on your work," the blonde said, "and you believe that the benefits outweigh the risks."

"Precisely. Researchers are considering going beyond transplanting a few isolated cells to creating chimeric animals with human brain regions. Other studies that transplanted human brain stem cells into monkeys' brains helped to launch a clinical trial to test whether human brain stem-cell transplants can treat Parkinson's disease. In many countries, including the United States and the United Kingdom, research that mixes human brain cells or tissue with another animal's brain is legally allowed and can be government funded with an extra layer of review."

"Wow!"

"What you've seen here is the beginning stage of this process," Perez said. "If you'll follow me to the next lab, I will show you how things have progressed through different stages of development."

With Rebecca close by his side, he led the group out of the lab, speaking as he went, down a hallway lined with windows to another lab where white-coated technicians milled around racks of animal cages and lab equipment.

"Researchers have been introducing human elements like organs, cells, or genes into other animals for decades to better understand how biological systems work and to find treatments for disease. Cancer researchers routinely transplant human tumors into mice and have created mice with human immune systems. We are also working to find ways to grow human-compatible organs in animals to alleviate the shortage of organs for transplantation."

"Pigs with human kidney or liver tissue are one thing," the heavy-set journalist with the short black curly hair and thick glasses asked, "but doesn't neural tissue raise different issues?"

Perez stopped and turned to the group with a raised finger. "It is the brain that people associate with moral status. None of the research to date even comes close to producing human-like cognition in an animal."

He turned back around and led the group through a door into a bigger more brightly lit windowed lab over to a dimly lit wall where three open topped oversized glass walled aquariums with different bar-coded tags with the letters A, B, and C attached to their fronts held small colonies of mice. An array of small digital cameras hung above, behind, and beside each of them covering every conceivable angle.

Rebecca brightened at the sight of the aquariums full of small toys that looked like props in a miniature lion tamer's cage. Mice groomed themselves and each other among stands and platforms of various heights, bridges, tiny swings, climbing ladders, seesaws, bell rollers, dumbbells, unicycles, and tree branches adorned with hanging twine.

 Some ran in hamster wheels, some sat up on their haunches nibbling away, and others chased each other around, sometimes letting out high-pitched squeaks. Tails wagged, whiskers wiggled, and a few stood up on hind legs with their ears pointed up and forward, watching the group gathered in front of them. Others burrowed under wood chip piles in the corners.

A large flat screen monitor hung above the aquariums showing revolving views, split screens, and closeups with letters designating which aquarium was being viewed along with information showing, date, time, magnification, and other data. "The mice in group A are our control group," Perez said.

Rebecca handed him a remote control which he pointed at the screen. "Each letter on the tanks designate the chronological progression of our experiments so far." He pressed the remote, showing a magnified image of the clump of human brain cells lighting up in flashes while settling into a living mouse brain that they had observed earlier.

"The brain organoids you are observing in action are self-organizing structures formed when brain stem cells are grown in three-dimensional culture. Some researchers have even stitched multiple organoids together into what we call assembloids. Organoids are complex enough to be a good way to ask questions about the human brain, but even assembloids are far from the complexity of the real thing because they lack sensory input, blood vessels, immune and support cells, and they don't receive feedback.

"Once the structures grow beyond 3–4 millimeters in size the cells in the middle die owing to lack of nutrients so it's hard to support their growth beyond a couple of months. To overcome these limitations, we are now transplanting organoids into an animal's brain to closely model the complexity of human brain circuits and how they go awry in disease." He pointed to the middle aquarium. "That brings us to group B."

Rebecca turned up the lights on the middle aquarium making it a little brighter than the others and the mice inside retreated a little toward the back of the aquarium.

"In group B lab-grown clumps of human brain cells were transplanted into the brains of newborn mice which grew into the rodents' own neural circuits, eventually making up around one-sixth of their brains. The brains of these young mice have undergone extensive growth and rewiring as they developed. Within four months their brain scans show that the organoids grew around nine times their original volume and made up around a third of one brain hemisphere. These cells have formed connections with mouse brain cells and have integrated into brain circuits."

Perez tapped the remote and a series of brain scan images shown from different perspectives, close ups, and short videos played across the screen as he spoke.

"Human neurons mature from an embryonic-like condition to a more complex state akin to neurons in an infant," Perez said, "and eventually show characteristics of adult neurons. Human brain tissue inserted into mouse brains grow blood vessels, mature, respond to stimuli, and form sparse working connections with mouse neurons. Human neurons in organoid transplants send long projections into the host brain which we hope will help us discover how this process differs between healthy human neurons and disease-affected neurons."

Rebecca perked up. "We hope that this research will lead to personalized organoid transplants that replace diseased or injured brain tissue."

"At what point does an animal's brain become too human-like for society's comfort?" the heavy-set journalist with thick glasses asked.

"Some people think that creating rodent–human hybrids could harm the animals or create animals with human-like brains, but human brain organoids are considered too primitive to become conscious, attain human-like intelligence, or acquire other abilities. Our organoid transplants have not caused problems like seizures or memory deficits in our mice and they haven't changed their behavior in any noticeable way. The grafted cells keep mostly to themselves and more than ninety percent of the connections they develop are human to human. They did send out projections to other parts of the mouse cortex and received a few projections, blood vessels, and immune cells from the mouse brain. This allowed the tissue to keep developing and playing out behavior normally expected in a developing human fetal brain like pruning neuronal branches and connections while starting to fire in coordinated waves."

"And their perceptions?" the petite blonde asked. "They might not become too human like, but could these transplants change the mouse's visual or sensory perception to a more human version?"

Rebecca looked to Perez, who winked, and they both smiled as if sharing an inside joke.

"Good question, m'dear," Perez said. "So far in group B, all of our mice have behaved like their non-transplanted peers but we believe that the limited numbers of human neurons and connections can change their outlook. We don't think stimulating even a few thousand human cells can drive human behavior or perception either." He held up a finger. "That brings us to group C!"

Rebecca dimmed the group B aquarium and Perez tapped the remote. The image of an active developing embryo filled the screen.

"Another way to study human brain development in a living organism is to add human ingredients or component parts into the earliest stages of another animal's developing embryo to make human–animal chimeric embryos so we can study organ development and one day grow organs for transplant."

Rebecca turned up the brightness on the group C aquarium and Perez tapped the remote showing a magnified image of dividing cells in the embryo onscreen, then he held his hand out toward the lit aquarium in a dramatic flourish.

"We added human stem cells to mice embryos within a few days of fertilization, when they were still just tiny balls of dividing cells. We have already been successful doing this with other rodents, livestock, and monkeys, which are more closely related to humans, but those chimeric embryos did not develop beyond their early stages or the human cells died off rapidly."

"We have greater hopes for the mice here in group C." Rebecca clapped her hands together like a little girl.

"When human cells are mixed into an embryo from the very beginning," Perez continued, "the organism typically fails to develop normally, but we are experimenting with a new process with human neural stem cells to see whether a piece of non-human primate brain can be grown in mice."

"Frankenmice," someone quipped causing the rest of the group to erupt in a half-hearted titter.

Perez chuckled. "When lab-grown clumps of human neurons are transplanted into newborn mice, they grow with the animals. These human neurons transplanted into a mouse's brain continue to grow, forming connections with the animals' own brain cells and helping to guide their behavior. One of the things we are monitoring closely is the unpredictable behavior of human embryonic cells placed into an animal embryo, and whether they might grow out of control. What's challenging is the uncertainty of what proportion might take over an embryo, but we are trusting the embryo to do its thing, although it might not be what we expect."

"Have you seen any physiological or any other behavioral changes in any of these mice?" the blonde girl asked.

"The cells themselves were much closer in size to neurons in human brains," Perez answered. "A few months after being transplanted, they were around six times bigger than those grown in a dish. They fire in a similar way to those in a human brain and they make up roughly one-third of a single hemisphere in a mouse brain. We injected the human tissue into the somatosensory cortexes of the mice where they receive and process sensory information like touch or pain."

"And in this case, you also believe that the ethical and moral implications outweigh the risks," the blonde said.

"Concerns about human organoids need to be weighed against the needs of people with neurological and psychiatric disorders. Brain organoids and human–animal hybrid brains could reveal the mechanisms underlying these illnesses, and they allow researchers to test therapies for conditions like schizophrenia and bipolar disorder. I think we have a responsibility as a society to do everything we can. If we have a way to save somebody's life or cure their disease, or provide some sort of therapy to minimize the pain or extend the life of the person, we should be allowed to exercise that."

He paused as if waiting for more questions, but none came, so he continued. "Now for what we call our crowning achievement."

Rebecca giggled.

"Right now he's somewhere in the back of the tank, so we don't want to disturb him, but our cameras have a constant eye on him."

Perez tapped the remote cycling through a series of camera views stopping at a close-up of a black mouse with a wet twitching nose and probing bright eyes that gave the impression of advanced intelligence. A device sat on top of its head with wires sticking out of it that resembled a crown.

"Allow me to introduce the star of our show, King!" Perez said with a dramatic gesture toward the screen. "King was anesthetized and implanted with stainless steel wires over the bilateral somatosensory and bilateral motor cortices. Reference wires were positioned over the cerebellum, and fiber optic implants were secured with dental cement. We genetically engineered the neurons in the organoids to fire when stimulated with light from the fiber-optic cables embedded in King's brain and trained him to lick a spout to receive water when the light was switched on. He now licks the spout in search of water whenever we stimulate the human neurons using blue light lasers. We also used a puff of air to prod his whiskers and discovered that more than seventy percent of the human neurons engaged in activity within a second or so of that stimulation." Perez's eyes lit up. "Eventually, this type of mouse model could be used to study psychiatric disorders, autism, or neurodegenerative diseases like Parkinson's or Alzheimer's and identify new treatments or test their effectiveness."

"And all of the other mice in group C have been implanted as embryos with the same human–animal chimeric embryos like King?" the blonde asked.

"Yes," Rebecca answered, "but he's the first to be crowned. We're waiting to see how the others evolve before fitting them with crowns at different stages of their development to track their evolution."

"What if things get out of control and they develop mutations, psychotic behaviors, or some other aberrant behavior?" the reporter asked. "Do you have a contingency plan?"

Perez looked down. "That's a good question and one we are prepared to deal with, but we are keeping a positive attitude. If something like that did arise, we would terminate them with carbon dioxide gas which is quick and humane, and it ensures that the mice would die immediately without any pain or suffering."

One morning a few months after the presentation Rebecca burst into Perez's office. "Doctor Perez," she said breathlessly. "You have to come to the lab right now!"

He rose from his desk. "What's the matter?"

"I don't know what to say. You have to see this!" She turned and left the office hurrying down the hallway with Perez in tow. She pushed open the door to the lab, hurried over to the group C aquarium, and flipped on the light.

Perez stopped mid-step and his mouth dropped open at the sight of all the mice in group C walking around on their hind legs like characters in some animated kid's show. He shook his head and rubbed his eyes in disbelief, then stepped forward for a closer look. King stood immobile at one end of the aquarium on top of one of the platforms as if overseeing the activity of all the other mice.

"How long has this been going on?" he finally managed.

"I don't know," Rebecca said. "I came in this morning and found them acting this way. I don't know what to make of it."

"Let's take a look at the video record," Perez said, grabbing the remote and looking up at the flat screen. He tapped the buttons, fast forwarding in reverse, stopping when the time date stamp on the video showed a shift in the activity of the mice, then he hit the play button. Going forward, the moment the timer digits hit midnight, King waddled out from the back of the enclosure on his hind legs, hopped up onto a platform and let out a series of high-pitched squeaks. One by one each of the mice rose up on their haunches and remained vertical.

"Fascinating," Perez said in a half-whisper.

"At midnight no less," Rebecca squealed. "It's like Cinderella's mice in reverse."

"Cinderella," Perez repeated. "I don't know what's happening here or what we'll discover when we investigate, but in the interim we'll call this the Cinderella Syndrome. We need to examine the brain of one of them right away, then terminate it and perform an autopsy to see if we can discover any clues about this behavior."

"We may have to terminate all of them if the National Academies of Science, Engineering and Medicine rule that it's too aberrant," Rebecca said.

"We want to avoid that at all costs," Perez said. "We need to keep this latest development under wraps, and restrict access to this part of the lab until further notice."

"I'll change the combinations on the door locks right away."

"Tell the others it's under quarantine and temporarily off limits because we suspect that there may be some kind of viral outbreak."

"Consider it done."

Less than an hour later Perez sat hunched over a microscope in a darkened laboratory while Rebecca gasped in disbelief watching large clumps of human brain cells in a mouse brain lighting up in accelerated flashes of activity on the monitor beside the microscope.

"Unbelievable," Perez half-whispered. "The grafted cells have sprouted new connections more than a few centimeters long and the majority of them have projected further into other parts of the mouse cortex. These structures are growing at an accelerated rate compared to developing human fetal brains and they are forming complex networks while firing in increasingly sophisticated coordinated waves."

"Should we be notifying anyone of this breakthrough?" Rebecca asked.

Perez held up a hand without looking up from the microscope. "I want to compile a more comprehensive data set before sharing this discovery, and I want to give it a little more time to see how things develop." He lowered his voice. "I'm also afraid that if we show too much too fast, we might get shut down."

"Agreed."

"We need to keep a very close eye on behaviors."

"That we will, and our video surveillance system will catch anything we might miss."

Rebecca showed up at Perez's office a couple of days later wide-eyed and red-faced. "Something new is happening," she said breathlessly.

Perez jumped up from his desk. "Jesus, are you alright? What is it?"

"It – it's – it's the mice in group C." She took a deep breath and blurted. "You're not going to believe this. You have to see it!"

She turned and hurried out of the office before Perez could respond, so he hustled after her. Her hands shook so bad, she couldn't punch in the lab combination code, so she stepped aside and let Perez do it, then she pushed past him and turned up the lights on the group C aquarium.

Perez froze at the surreal scene playing out in front of him, then he closed his eyes and shook his head, refusing to believe what he saw.

The stands, platforms, bridges, swings, ladders, seesaws, bell rollers, dumbbells, unicycles, and tree branches with hanging twine that looked like lion tamer's props were arranged in a circle resembling an obstacle course around the circumference of the aquarium.

King stood at one end of the aquarium on the highest platform looking royally black, adorned with his wired crown. His wet twitching nose and bright eyes accented the impression of him as a ringmaster waving his paws like an orchestra conductor overseeing numerous acrobatic feats while the other mice responded to his squeaking commands. With each loud squeak his subject mice moved successively forward like a precision clockwork mechanism through each of the toys that made up the course.

Neither Perez nor Rebecca spoke for a long minute until Rebecca broke the silence.

"There's something else happening too."

Perez blinked as if waking from a trance.

Rebecca grabbed the remote and cycled through a few camera views until they showed a closeup of the corners of the aquarium where mice burrowed under wood chip piles that seemed to move with a life of their own.

"I did an inventory and discovered that the mice in group C are reproducing at twice the rate of the other two groups."

Perez came to life as if prodded by an electric shock. "That could be an indicator of bigger problems. Grab one of the pups so we can see what might be developing in this next generation."

"Right away."

Perez peered into the microscope in the darkened laboratory watching the cells inside the pup's brain erupting like fourth of July fireworks while Rebecca watched spellbound on the monitor. The image looked nearly identical to a human brain in miniature which was more human than mouse, but definitely hybrid.

"I don't believe what I am seeing," Perez said.

"I wouldn't believe it either if I wasn't seeing myself," Rebecca added.

"Almost full domination of the mouse cortex, including blood vessels and immune cells growing at an accelerated rate forming complex networks, pruning neuronal branches and connections, all firing in coordinated waves identical to those of a developing human."

He looked up from the microscope. "As much as I am hesitant to share what is happening, the rapid pace of this progression has advanced to the point where we have to report it to the National Academies of Science, Engineering and Medicine. I need you to copy all the relevant video records while I write up a report which I will submit to them this afternoon with the greatest of urgency."

"Will do!"

Perez called Rebecca and had her meet him in his office later that evening. "The National Academies board of directors don't believe my report or the videos and they are accusing me of doctoring the videos to perpetrate a hoax. They'll be here in a few minutes to personally observe these phenomena and advise us on the proper actions. I fear the worst, but we are working under the directives of their ethics committee and we need to toe the line when it comes to their recommendations."

Rebecca sighed. "I dread what they will order us to do, which will be a shame." She shook her head. "I still can't believe what's happening, but we can't deny what we are seeing."

Perez's phone rang and he snatched it up on the first ring. "Yes," he said nodding. "Escort them directly to the lab and we'll meet them there."

Three sullen faced men met him and Rebecca outside the lab.

"This better be good," a white-haired conservatively dressed man who introduced himself as professor Jenkins said.

"You won't be disappointed," Rebecca said.

Perez punched in the combination and led the delegation over to group three's aquarium where they could see the mice walking upright on their hind legs in the semidarkness. Jenkins gasped and his two associates remained silent.

Rebecca turned up the aquarium lights and King marched out of the shadows on queue looking regal with his wired crown as if a curtain had been raised on a show's opening. He took his place on the raised platform at the end of the aquarium and let out a series of high-pitched squeals while waving his orchestra conductor paws. The rest of the mice fell into place following his commands, moving successively forward in their precision clockwork dance making their way through each of the toys on the circular course.

"My god," Jenkins muttered. "It's real!"

His two associates leaned in and one of them said. "I wouldn't believe it I wasn't seeing it myself."

They all watched in silence for a few minutes before Jenkins said, "And the mice in this group are reproducing at twice the rate of the other two groups?"

"That's correct," Rebecca said.

Jenkins shook his head slowly. "Amazing! It's bittersweet but we have no choice but to terminate the entire colony. We can't let this aberration continue. There are too many unknowns and variables, but on the plus side we can share samples for other labs to autopsy and analyze."

Perez sighed and stared down at the floor. "I know that was going to be your conclusion, but I understand. We'll get some CO_2 tanks up here and eradicate the whole population first thing in the morning. The other positive in this otherwise painful termination is that we have extensive records of our lab work and hours of in-depth video monitoring from every possible perspective."

"So it's not a total loss," Jenkins said, patting him on the shoulder. "I'll expect a full report by close of business tomorrow." He looked wistfully at the performing mice for a few moments longer, then turned away and walked out the door in silence with his associates in tow.

Perez looked up when Rebecca came through his office door early the next morning looking downtrodden. "I had the CO_2 tank delivered outside the lab this morning. I am not going to enjoy doing this."

Perez came around from behind his desk. "I understand. I've grown attached to them myself, but we can't argue with the ruling. They have the authority to shut us down completely for noncompliance. If it's any comfort to you, you don't have to assist me. I can handle it myself."

"No," she said wistfully. "I've been with them from the start. I want to follow through until the end."

"No sense in dragging it out then. Let's get it over with." He patted her on the shoulder and led her out of the office, speaking as they walked down the hall. "We'll seal off the aquariums and gas them at high pressure to get it over with quickly with minimum suffering and trauma on their part. We'll have to exterminate all three groups so there are no questions. We'll rig it up so that it all happens simultaneously."

"Agreed."

Perez grabbed the CO_2 tank and Rebecca held the door open while he rolled it in.

"What the…" He stopped short in front of Rebecca and she stumbled into him.

She caught herself from falling over and stared dumbfounded, then moving as if in a trance she turned up the lights on the aquariums.

Toys covered the tops of the aquariums, including the stands, platforms, bridges, swings, ladders, seesaws, hamster wheels, rollers, dumbbells, unicycles, and tree branches creating pathways down into each aquarium. Every piece linked together in a sophisticated arrangement of devices that connected everything to a longer improvised pathway on one side that ended at the floor.

No trace of mice from the other groups remained in any of the aquariums, including the babies.

HOW MAD MAX WON
THE NOBEL PRIZE IN LITERATURE

Max, known as "Mad Max" to his friends because of his obsession with writing, shuffled into Harry's Plaza Cafe clutching a dog-eared manuscript under his arm. *I'm never going to sell this piece of shit*, he thought. *Why do I even bother to keep submitting it?*

"Because you believe in your work," a voice in his head said.

It sounded so close and so real that he spun around to see who spoke, but saw no one. He felt a mild chill.

Fuck, I'm losing it.

He eyed the long bar and saw a slender, attractive long-legged blonde at the end of it and decided to check her out and maybe escape his misery in her company, so he started toward her. Half way down the length of the bar he tripped, feeling as if someone had stuck their foot out causing him to lose his balance. Floundering, he fell forward onto a bar stool which kept him from hitting the floor and by some miracle he managed to hang on to his manuscript.

He yanked his hands back, thinking it odd that the seat of the bar stool felt warm, as if someone had been sitting there. He saw the indent of two butt cheeks that did not come from him, but saw no drink on the bar. He straightened and glanced sideways, mortified to see the blonde putting her hand over her mouth to hide a smile.

Shit, blew that chance.

A silver-haired bartender with a handlebar mustache leaned toward him on the bar. "You okay buddy?"

"Yeah, sure," Max said. "Sorry I should have paid more attention to where I put my feet."

The bartender glanced sideways down the bar at the blonde and winked. "Don't blame ya!" He slapped a napkin down on the bar. "What can I get you?"

Max snuck one last glance at the blonde, then said, "Fuck it! I'll have a Mai Tai."

"You got it!"

Max took a seat beside the warm one, put his manuscript on the bar, and looked at the ass impressions which looked really out of place. After the bartender brought his Mai Tai, Max reached out tentatively and pulled his hand back as if burned when he felt the seat. Still warm! *What the fu…*

"Drink up," the voice he heard at the door said.

He looked around again, seeing nobody, thinking he recognized the voice from years back. Too weird! He took a long sip from his drink. *That ought to shut it up.*

He finished the Mai Tai, feeling its affects calming him and was about to summon the bartender for another when the voice said, "Well m'boy, try a Rum and Coke, my favorite, and maybe we'll see about getting you some help with that sorry looking manuscript you keep dragging around. You look like a sad, lost little puppy."

Max looked behind him, then to both sides and could swear he saw the ass impression on the seat beside him dimpling, like someone sat there. He reached out grabbing at the air above the bar stool in a big sweeping gesture as if to pull it close and half fell over, looking up to see the cute blonde looking straight at him with a puzzled expression. She gave him a grimacing half-smile and a half-hearted three finger wave.

Shit!

With a short nod to her he sat up looking straight ahead, focusing all of his attention on the empty Mai Tai glass. He wanted to order another, but what came out of his mouth was, "Bartender! Rum and Coke please."

When it came he took an extended first sip.

"Atta boy. Stick with me. My friends and I will help you out."

"Jeez," Max whispered, "not at the rate I'm going." He took another long sip from the Rum and Coke. "You sound like Ernest Hemingway."

"Stick with your Uncle Ernie," the voice said, confirming his realization. "Now drink up m'boy, we have work to do."

Max took another long sip, draining the glass, feeling the alcohol driving him deeper. He forgot about the cute blonde and put all his attention on the voice of Hemingway that spoke to him from somewhere inside of his head, then he closed his eyes and abandoned himself to wherever Hemingway was going to take him.

"I know you write science fiction," Hemingway said. "Order a Vodka and Tonic and Bradbury will come and give us his advice."

"Bartender!" Max said without hesitation, "Vodka and Tonic please."

"You're putting them away pretty fast there, buddy," the bartender said. "You sure you want to..."

"Don't worry about it." Max waved him off. "This one's not for me. It's for a friend who will be here in a minute."

"You got it!" the bartender said.

"Listen, don't worry about what other people think," Ray Bradbury's distinctive voice boomed in his head when the Vodka and Tonic came. "Write for the love of it I tell you!"

Max's eyes popped open and he half-expected to see Bradbury sitting beside him pointing a finger to make his point. The blonde had gone and the bartender busied himself at a sink washing glasses, so Max closed his eyes again.

Someone shook him and Hemingway said, "Are you paying attention to what he said?"

Max looked across a round table at Ray Bradbury, who smiled from behind thick Coke bottle bottom glasses. To Ray's left sat F. Scott Fitzgerald, William Faulkner, J.R.R. Tolkien, Dashiell Hammett, and Jonathan Winters. Hemingway sat beside Max to his left, completing the circle. They all had manuscripts that they scribbled on with red pens. Dumbfounded, Max looked around, recognizing a meeting room in the back of Harry's where they were known to have met. He had been there a few times himself with his writing group.

"Don't you think it would be a better story with a female protagonist," Tolkien said as he continued writing in red.

"My Aunt Maude thinks it could be a lot funnier," Jonathan Winters said in an old lady voice with exaggerated facial expressions that matched the voice.

"It can definitely use more suspense," Faulkner said with a Southern accent. His eyes twinkled and a broad smile accented by his bushy mustache filled his face. He tipped his hat to Max before going back to writing on the manuscript.

"If you really want to make it sing, "Hammett added, "you might want to consider adding more noir elements to it. He nodded to

Faulkner and winked. "It'll help you address the suspense part that Bill is looking for."

The discussion went on from there discussing scene setting, characterization, plotting, pacing, structure, and other critical elements of storytelling. Everyone had their own ideas, opinions, and approaches, and everyone made copious notes in red on their respective manuscripts.

"Pay attention, m'boy," Hemingway said, giving Max another shake. "This is your big chance." He winked. "My money's on you!"

Max shook more and felt himself slowly sitting up, like waking from some kind of weird dream. Forcing his eyes open, he looked up into the concerned face of the bartender.

"Hey, you OK buddy? Want me to call an Uber for you?"

Max looked around, blinking. He was the only one left in Harry's and the lights were getting turned off. "Sure, Max said. "Thank you."

In what seemed like the next moment he awoke in bed with a pounding headache, aggravated by the bright sunlight. His manuscript sat neatly stacked on his nightstand. He stumbled out of bed to close the shades and lost his balance, knocking the manuscript off the nightstand in a flurry of pages.

He stepped through the scattered pages to close the shades and shut out the blazing agony and went back to drop down on the bed to stare at the mess on the floor when the red ink caught his eye.

He closed his eyes and shook his head as if to clear them and sank down to the floor looking from page to page, seeing red on every page of the manuscript written in six different kinds of handwriting.

BLINDED BY THE LIGHT

Jesus and Satan appeared before the Lord God Almighty, who is worshipped by a great portion of humanity as the omniscient omnipresent Creator who encompasses all things in the known and unknown Universe, including Heaven, Hell, and every degree of conceivable light and darkness imaginable.

The heavenly abode of the Source of all that is, is characterized as the land of peace, love, and abundance flowing with milk and honey with pearly gates at its entrance, serenading angels and cherubim, magnificent streets, and structures of gold. Heaven is believed to be a cosmological, transcendent place where gods, angels, spirits, saints, or revered ancestors are said to originate, be enthroned, or live. Depending on the multitude of beliefs that the various tribes of humanity have evolved in, the most common element underlying Heaven and Hell is the concept of reward, punishment, and redemption.

In truth, these conceptions barely hint at a greater reality that defies the limitations of simplistic human thought because the infinite heart of the Source exists beyond any comprehensible conception of space and time. The spirits of Satan and his beloved brother Jesus basked in the awesome power of a radiance so pure as to be incomprehensible to mere mortals. They were among the very few who could withstand the intensity of the light from the Almighty who radiated all-consuming unconditional love direct from the Source.

From within the presence of the Great Mystery the voice of the Almighty rang out from the infinite depths of its dazzling brilliance like the low rumble of thunder, permeating the two brothers to the core of their being in wordless emanations of luminous energy that came from everywhere.

"You are my first division characterized as emissaries of Heaven, Hell, and all activity both good and bad perpetrated by humanity, yet you are undivided at your essence. Symbolically, you are the manifestation of the light *and* the dark, which are one and the same light that *I Am* making you the complementary poles of the Great Mystery. Regardless of humanity's many beliefs and misguided conceptions of the true nature of the light and the darkness, you two are the primary bearers of my light."

"I understand," Lucifer said in the same telepathic manner. "According to the myths that I am credited with, my purpose is to separate the children of darkness from the children of light and I serve willingly, and though I am in your service, I am to blame for humanity's sins."

"Though the myths regarding my time on Earth are much shorter than the eternal endurance of Lucifer," Jesus added, "my legacy continues."

"Not only has it continued," the Creator's voice boomed from its directionless source, "but it has multiplied into an infinite number of beliefs that mankind has created around your incarnation."

"In spite of your short time on Earth," Lucifer said, "the breadth and depth of your mythology rivals mine."

Jesus brightened. "And they have combined our myths and made us bitter adversaries."

The Creator laughed, filling everything with an unearthly sound somewhere between the peal of bells and the tinkling of wind chimes that sounded nothing like either one of them. "My two brightest lights who I have tasked with the same mission have become adversaries in the eyes of humanity."

"I am considered the Alpha and the Omega", Jesus said. "The beginning and the end, which is interpreted by many Christians to mean that I have existed for all eternity like Lucifer and I am credited with being an incarnation of God eternal while many who are swallowed in darkness believe that Lucifer represents the end."

"Make no mistake," the voice of the Mystery said. "In spite of all the confusion, you serve me in a sacred task as my ambassadors of light, but for the most part humanity fears the light and embraces the darkness."

"And all of this comes from the imagination," Satan said.

The Creator's voice reverberated through them all. "Heaven is described as a higher place and is considered to be the holiest place and a Paradise in contrast to Hell, the Underworld which is thought to be universally accessible by earthly beings according to varying standards of divinity, goodness, piety, faith, or other virtues, right beliefs, or simply My will."

The light of Jesus brightened. "The myth of my resurrection says that I ascended to Heaven where I sit at your right hand and will return to earth in the Second Coming."

"I suppose there is some grain of truth to that, the Creator said, "as you are here with me now along with Lucifer." "That is true," Satan said, "but the greater truth is that we have never left your side."

"We are devoted to you," Jesus added.

"A key element attributed to you, Jesus," Satan continued, "talks about a war in Heaven between Michael the Archangel and his angels against me and my angels, ending with me and my angels being thrown down to the earth."

"There are also reports of negative life-reviews that share the concept of Hell," Jesus said, "as a place of torment and punishment located in another dimension or under the Earth's surface. In many religious cultures Hell is fiery, painful, and harsh, inflicting suffering on the guilty. Other traditions describe it as cold."

A hint of a heavenly sigh passed through them before the Creator spoke again. "This is the very definition of necessary evil which is designed to purify My light within the souls of humanity, but this is done in a manner quite different from the simplistic split between the good and evil of light and dark that humanity blindly clings to."

Satan chuckled. "According to legends I am credited with, my name Lucifer is connected to the planet Venus and this name was absorbed into Christianity as a name for the devil. There is a Bible passage from Isaiah, where I am referred to as morning star or shining one. In Roman folklore, Lucifer, is light-bringer, and in Latin it was the name of the planet Venus, but I wasn't any goddess of beauty and love. They personified me as a male bearing a torch. The Greek name for Venus was Phosphoros which also means light-bringer, or Heosphoros, dawn-bringer, and they often spoke of me in poetry as heralding the dawn."

"It never ceases to amaze me," Jesus said, "how much they fear the light. So much so, that they twisted something as beautiful as an emissary of light from the Source and turned into something vile, distorted, and opposite."

Satan's light brightened in response. "Considering pride as a major sin of self-deification, Lucifer became the template for the devil and is identified with the devil in Christianity. Early medieval Christianity distinguished between Lucifer and Satan. While Lucifer, as the devil, is fixated in hell, Satan executes the desires of Lucifer as his vassal. Theologians made no distinction between Lucifer and Satan. They regarded Lucifer as Satan's primordial name."

A subtle cosmic chuckle rumbled through them all before the voice of the Great Mystery Spoke again. "Many versions of the bible, which is supposed to be the definitive record of *My* word translate morning star as Lucifer, son of the morning. Isaiah wrote about Satan's fall from heaven and the morning star refers to Satan. I would never cast down anyone from my presence. That is not unconditional love. Any banishment from the light is self-imposed through fear of the light. To add to the confusion of what is supposedly My word, Jesus identifies Himself as the morning star in Revelation." These last words echoed into a brief silence, then, "This begs the question, why are the both of you described as the morning star?"

The stories about me are mind boggling," Satan added, "and they blamed me for a lot of darkness. Augustine of Hippo's work from the 5th century, *Civitas Dei* became the major opinion of Western demonology. Augustine said that my rebellion was the first and final cause of evil. He rejected earlier teachings about me having fallen when the world was already created and he rejected the idea that envy was the first sin where I supposedly fell because I envied humans and refused to prostrate myself before Adam. Augustine argued that evil first came into existence by my free will which made me a scapegoat who tried to take God's throne and become God. When the King of Babel spoke in Isaiah, he was said to be speaking through my spirit as the head of devils when he concluded that everyone who falls away from God are within my body, and is a devil."

The light of the Creator brightened. "There is a kernel of truth in this because I am omniscient. I exist within Lucifer and Lucifer exists within me. I am eternal and exist within all as all exist within me."

"Some of them did manage to get it right," Satan said, "but they have mostly been ignored. Luciferianism is inspired by the teachings of Gnosticism and reveres me not as the devil, but as a savior, a guardian or instructing spirit, or even the true god. In *The Satanic Bible*, Lucifer is one of the four crown princes of hell, particularly that of the East, the lord of the air, and I am called the bringer of light, the morning star, intellectualism, and enlightenment. When Freemasons and Masonic scholars spoke about the energies of Lucifer, they were referring to the Morning Star, the light bearer, the search for light; the very antithesis of dark. The Freemason Albert Pike said in Morals and Dogma, 'Lucifer, the Son of the Morning! Is it *he* who bears the Light, and with its splendors intolerable blinds feeble, sensual, or selfish Souls? Doubt it not!'"

"There is truth in that too," the Creator's voice rang out, "but it has nearly been extinguished by the elaborate tapestry of the human imagination's fear of that very light. Your identity as Satan began as an entity in the Abrahamic religions who seduces humans into sin. In Christianity and Islam you are seen as a fallen angel who possessed great piety and beauty who rebelled against Me, and those lost souls believe that I still allow you power over the fallen world and a host of demons. In Judaism, you are a metaphor for the evil inclination as an agent subservient to Me. Your identity as *the* satan first appeared in the Hebrew Bible as a Heavenly prosecutor, and a member of My sons of God under the name Yahweh who prosecuted the nation of Judah in the Heavenly court and tested the loyalty of My followers by forcing them to suffer.

"In the time between the Hebrew Bible and the Christian New Testament the idea of Satan developed into a malevolent entity with abhorrent qualities in opposition to Me." The Creator chortled with an otherworldly echo. "In the Book of Jubilees I supposedly grant you authority over a group of fallen angels to tempt humans to sin and punish them. In the Synoptic Gospels you tempt Jesus in the desert and are identified as the cause of illness and temptation. In the Book of Revelation you appear as a Great Red Dragon who is defeated by Michael the Archangel, cast down from Heaven, and bound for a thousand years until set free before being defeated and cast into the Lake of Fire."

"So much for unconditional love," Jesus quipped.

"In Christianity, Satan is known as the Devil," the Creator continued, "and although the Book of Genesis doesn't mention you, you are often identified as the serpent in the Garden of Eden. In medieval times you played a minimal role in Christian theology and were used as a comic relief figure in mystery plays, but your significance increased as beliefs in widespread demonic possession and witchcraft became more prevalent. During the Age of Enlightenment belief in the existence of Satan became harshly criticized, but this belief has persisted, particularly in the Americas.

"In the Quran, Shaitan, also known as Iblis is an entity made of fire who was cast out of Heaven because he refused to bow before the newly created Adam and incited humans and jinn to sin by infecting their minds with evil suggestions and in Theistic Satanism, Satan is a deity who is either worshipped or revered. In LaVeyan Satanism, Satan is a symbol of virtuous characteristics and liberty."

"It makes me sound bipolar, Satan said, "but you hardly ever hear anything virtuous about me. Humanity enjoys the drama of doom, gloom, and hellfire more."

"Your darker reputation precedes you," Jesus said.

"The original Hebrew term *sâtan* is a noun meaning accuser or adversary," the Creator continued, "which is used throughout the Hebrew Bible to refer to human adversaries as well as a specific supernatural entity. The word is derived from a verb meaning to obstruct or oppose. When it was used as simply *satan*, it referred to any accuser, but when it was used specifically as *ha-satan*, it referred to the heavenly accuser, *the* Satan. The word satan isn't in the Book of Genesis which only mentions a talking serpent. It doesn't identify the serpent with any supernatural entity, but Satan appears in the Book of Job, a righteous man favored by my identity as Yahweh who asks one of the sons of God known as Satan, where he has been.

"Satan says that he has been roaming around the earth, then Yahweh asks, 'Have you considered My servant Job?' Satan replies by urging Yahweh to let him torture Job, promising that Job will abandon his faith at the first tribulation. Yahweh consents and Satan destroys Job's servants and flocks, but Job refuses to condemn Yahweh. Yahweh points out Job's continued faithfulness and Satan insists on more testing. Yahweh once again gives him permission but in the end Job remains faithful and righteous, and it is implied that Satan is shamed in his defeat."

"Though nothing could be further from the truth, " Jesus said, "You have to give them credit for their wild imaginations. The idea of Satan as my opponent and a purely evil figure came from Jewish writings from the Second Temple Period, particularly in the *apocalypses*. The Book of Enoch, which the Dead Sea Scrolls have revealed to have been nearly as popular as the Torah describes a group of two hundred angels known as the Watchers assigned to supervise the earth, who abandon their duties and have sexual intercourse with human women. The Watchers are ultimately sequestered in isolated caves across the earth condemned to face judgment at the end of time. The Book of Jubilees, written around one-hundred-fifty BC retells the story of the Watchers' defeat that is different from the Book of Enoch. In it

Mastema, an angel who persecutes evil in Jewish mythology carries out punishments for Me as well as tempting humans and testing their faith. In the Zadokite Fragments and the Dead Sea Scrolls he is the angel of disaster, the father of all evil, and a flatterer of God who first appears in the literature of the Second Temple Period as a personification of the Hebrew word *mastemah* meaning hatred, hostility, enmity, or persecution."

Lucifer chuckled. "You have to admit, I was becoming more omniscient and moved beyond being simply bipolar to a multiple personality."

"That you did," the Creator said. "In Christianity the most common English synonym for Satan is devil and in the New Testament, the words *Satan* and *diabolos* are used interchangeably. Beelzebub, meaning Lord of Flies, is the name given in the Hebrew Bible and New Testament to a Philistine god whose original name has been reconstructed as Ba'al Zabul, meaning Baal the Prince. The Synoptic Gospels identify Satan and Beelzebub as the same. The name Abaddon, meaning place of destruction is used six times in the Old Testament mainly as a name for a region of Sheol. Revelation describes Abaddon, which translates into Greek as *Apollyon*, meaning the destroyer, as an angel who rules the Abyss.

"In later Christianity Satan is never referred to without mentioning Jesus. The three Synoptic Gospels all describe the temptation of Christ by Satan in the desert where he first showed Jesus a stone and told him to turn it into bread, then he took Jesus to the pinnacle of the Temple in Jerusalem and commanded him to throw himself down so the angels would catch him. After that Satan took Jesus to the top of a tall mountain and showed him the kingdoms of the earth, promising to give them all to him if he bowed down and worshiped him. Jesus denied Satan every time and after the third temptation he was saved by the angels."

"You sure did get around," Jesus added. "You even made it into my mythologies!"

"Indeed," the Creator said. "Satan also played a role in some of your parables. According to the Parable of the Sower, Satan influenced those who failed to understand the gospel. Other parables said that Satan's followers would be punished on Judgment Day with the Parable of the Sheep and the Goats stating that the Devil, his angels, and the people who followed him would be consigned to eternal fire. When the Pharisees accused Jesus of exorcising demons through the power of Beelzebub, Jesus told them, 'how can someone enter a strong man's house and plunder his goods, unless he first binds the strong man? Then indeed he may plunder his house.' The strong man in this parable was Satan."

"They finally connected us as one and the same light," Jesus said, "but in their love of the darkness the Pharisees decided to make *you* work through *me*! I guess they needed a scapegoat and had a real attachment to that whole bipolar identity. The Synoptic Gospels identify you and your demons as the causes of illness, including fever and arthritis while the Epistle to the Hebrews describe the Devil as him who holds the power of death. They put me back in charge again in Luke where they say I granted you the authority to test Peter and the other apostles and Judas who betrayed me because you entered him.

"In the Gospel of John, he wrote that I said that the Jews are the children of the Devil rather than the children of Abraham. The same verse describes the Devil as a man-killer from the beginning and the father of lying. John identified you as the Archon of this Cosmos who is destined to be overthrown through my death and resurrection."

"We saw how that turned out," Lucifer said.

"John also promised that the Holy Spirit would accuse the world of sin, justice, and judgment," Jesus said, "a role that resembled Satan in the Old Testament."

Lucifer's glow brightened. "My appeal grew from there as did my reputation and the colorful descriptions of my power and manifestations. Revelation describes a Great Red Dragon with seven heads, ten horns, seven crowns, and a massive tail, an image inspired by the vision of the four beasts from the sea in the Book of Daniel and the Leviathan described in the Old Testament. The Great Red Dragon knocks a third of the sun, a third of the moon, and a third of the stars out of the sky and pursues the Woman of the Apocalypse.

"In Revelation war broke out in Heaven and Michael and his angels fought against Dragon and his angels who were beaten and there was no longer any place for them in Heaven, then a voice boomed down from Heaven heralding the defeat of the Accuser, identifying the Satan of Revelation with the Satan of the Old Testament. Satan is bound with a chain and hurled into the Abyss where he is imprisoned for a thousand years, then set free to gather his armies along with Gog and Magog to wage war against the righteous, but is defeated with fire from Heaven and cast into the lake of fire."

"There's that lake of fire again," the Creator snorted, "and hurled into the Abyss and set free again. You have to admit, they can't seem to get enough of you! Early Christians believed that you gained power over humanity through Adam and Eve's sin, and Christ's death on the cross was considered a ransom to you in exchange for humanity's liberation. This myth says that Satan was tricked by God because Christ was not only free of sin, but was the incarnate Deity who Satan lacked the ability to enslave.

"Most early Christians believed that Satan and his demons could possess humans and exorcisms were widely practiced by Jews, Christians, and pagans. Belief in demonic possession continued through the Middle Ages when exorcisms were seen as a display of God's power over Satan. Most people who thought they were possessed by the Devil didn't suffer from hallucinations or other spectacular symptoms. They complained of anxiety, religious fears, and evil thoughts. Christians regarded Satan as increasingly powerful and the fear of his power became a dominant aspect of Christian worldview.

"Early English settlers of North America, especially the Puritans, believed that Satan reigned in the New World. John Winthrop claimed that the Devil made rebellious Puritan women give birth to stillborn monsters with claws, sharp horns, and on each foot three claws, like a young fowl. Cotton Mather wrote that devils swarmed around Puritan settlements like the frogs of Egypt. The Puritans believed that Native Americans were worshippers of Satan and described them as children of the Devil, and some settlers claimed to have seen Satan appear in the flesh at native ceremonies. During the First Great Awakening, the new light preachers portrayed their old light critics as ministers of Satan. By the time of the Second Great Awakening, Satan's primary role in American evangelicalism was the opponent of the evangelical movement itself. They said that he spent most of his time trying to hinder the ministries of evangelical preachers, a role he has largely retained among present-day American fundamentalists."

Jesus let out a low otherworldly whistle. "Satan sure was popular in those days! He consorted with witches who were believed to fly through the air on broomsticks. He also consorted with demons, performed in lurid sexual rituals in the forests, murdered human infants and ate them as part of Satanic rites, and he engaged in conjugal relations with demons."

"The devil made me do it," Satan joked.

Jesus suppressed a giggle. "The panic over witchcraft intensified in the sixteen-twenties and continued until the end of the sixteen-hundreds. Around sixty-thousand people were executed for witchcraft during the witchcraft hysteria."

"All in My name, no less," the Creator boomed. "By the eighteenth century trials for witchcraft ended in most western countries with the exceptions of Poland and Hungary, but belief in the power of Satan remained strong among Christians. Belief in Satan and demonic possession still remains strong among Christians in the United States and Latin America. Most American Christians don't separate what they know about Satan from the movies, from what they know from theological traditions. The Catholic Church played down Satan and exorcism during the late twentieth century, but Pope Francis brought renewed focus on the Devil in the early twenty-first century stating that, 'The devil is intelligent, he knows more theology than all the theologians together.'

"Christianity views Satan as a mythological attempt to express the reality and extent of evil in the universe existing outside and apart from humanity, but influencing human experience, still another way of blaming everything but themselves for their choices. In the dualist approach Satan will become incarnate in the Antichrist, just as God became incarnate in Jesus, but in Orthodox Christian thought this view is a problem because it is too similar to Christ's incarnation. Instead, the Antichrist is a human figure inhabited by Satan since Satan's power is not seen as equal to God's, but in truth it is, because I am in *everything*."

"Atheistic Satanism practiced by the Satanic Temple and by followers of LaVeyan Satanism say that I don't exist as an anthropomorphic entity," Lucifer said, "but as a symbol of a cosmos that satanists perceive to be permeated and motivated by a force that has been given many names over the course of time. In this religion I am not seen as a hubristic, irrational, fraudulent creature, but I am revered with Prometheus-like attributes, symbolizing liberty and individual empowerment, which *is* closer to the truth.

"I also serve as a conceptual framework and an external metaphorical projection of the satanist's highest personal potential. A High Priest of the Church of Satan stated that I am a symbol of Man living as his prideful, carnal nature dictates, and that the reality behind me is simply the dark evolutionary force of entropy that permeates all of nature and provides the drive for survival and propagation inherent in all living things. I am not thought of as a conscious entity to be worshiped, but a reservoir of power inside each human to be tapped at will. The Church of Satan chose me as its primary symbol because in Hebrew Satan means adversary, opposer, and one to accuse or question. They see themselves as being these Satans, the adversaries, opposers, and accusers of all spiritual belief systems that try to hamper enjoyment of their lives as human beings."

Jesus sighed. "Those poor healers and herbalists who were scapegoated as witches. Wicca has evolved into a modern day religion whose practitioners Christians have incorrectly assumed to worship Satan. Wiccans don't believe in the existence of Satan or anything like him. Much folklore about satanism doesn't originate from the beliefs or practices of theistic or atheistic satanists, but from a mixture of medieval Christian folk beliefs, conspiracy theories, and urban legends. Modern times weren't any better. The satanic ritual abuse scare of the nineteen-eighties depicted satanism as a vast conspiracy of elites with a predilection for child abuse and human sacrifice backed by the thought of Satan physically incarnating to receive worship."

"More scapegoating," Satan added.

"In Dante's *Inferno*," Jesus continued, "Satan appears as a giant demon frozen mid-breast in ice at the center of the Ninth Circle of Hell with three faces and a pair of bat-like wings affixed under each chin. In his three mouths he gnaws on Brutus, Judas Iscariot, and Cassius, whom Dante regarded as having betrayed the two greatest heroes of the human race; Julius Caesar, the founder of the new order of government, and me, the founder of the new order of religion. As Satan beats his wings he creates a cold wind that continues to freeze the ice surrounding him and the other sinners in the Ninth Circle. Satan also appeared in several stories from *The Canterbury Tales* by Geoffrey Chaucer, including *The Summoner's Prologue*, where a friar arrives in Hell and sees no other friars but is told there are millions, then Satan lifts his tail to reveal that all of the friars live inside his anus. Chaucer's description of Satan's appearance is based on Dante's.

"The legend of Faust recorded in fifteen-eighty-nine concerns a pact allegedly made by the German scholar Johann Georg Faust with a demon named Mephistopheles agreeing to sell his soul to Satan in exchange for twenty-four years of earthly pleasure. John Milton's epic poem *Paradise Lost* features Satan as a tragic antihero destroyed by his own hubris who dares to rebel against the tyranny of God in spite of God's omnipotence. *Paradise Regained*, the sequel to *Paradise Lost*, is a retelling of Satan's temptation of Jesus in the desert.

"On a positive note, William Blake regarded Satan as a model of rebellion against unjust authority and featured him in many of his poems and illustrations including his book *The Marriage of Heaven and Hell*, where Satan is celebrated as the ultimate rebel, the incarnation of human emotion, and the epitome of freedom from all forms of reason and orthodoxy. Based on the Biblical passages portraying Satan as the accuser of sin, Blake interpreted him as a promulgator of moral laws. Satan's appearance is never described in the Bible or any early Christian writings, though Paul the Apostle did write that 'Satan disguises himself as an angel of light.' The Devil was never shown in early Christian artwork. He first appeared in medieval art of the ninth century with cloven hooves, hairy legs, the tail of a goat, pointed ears, a beard, a flat nose, and horns. Much of Satan's descriptions in Christianity were stolen from Pan, the goat-legged fertility god in ancient Greek religion.

"Early Christian writers equated the Greek satyrs and the Roman fauns that Pan resembled with demons, and the Devil's pitchfork appears to have been adapted from the trident wielded by the Greek god Poseidon, while Satan's flame-like hair seems to have originated from the Egyptian god Bes. By the High Middle Ages Satan and devils appeared in all works of Christian art including paintings, sculptures, and cathedrals and is usually depicted naked, but his genitals are rarely shown and often covered by animal furs. The goat-like portrayal of Satan was closely associated with him in his role as the object of worship by sorcerers and as the incubus, a demon believed to rape women in their sleep.

"How flattering," Satan said in a monotone. "A rapist emissary of light no less."

"Talk about a bad rap and a literal scapegoat," the Creator rumbled. "Aside from all the heinous behavior attributed to him, Satan is embodied with goat qualities like fur, hooves, and goat legs. Italian frescoes from the late Middle Ages show him chained in Hell feeding on the bodies of the perpetually damned and as the serpent in the Garden of Eden. He is often shown as a snake with arms and legs as well the head and full-breasted upper torso of a woman. Satan and his demons could take any form in medieval art, and demons were shown as short, hairy, black-skinned humanoids with clawed bird feet and extra faces on their chests, bellies, genitals, buttocks, and tails.

"By now it should be clear that Lucifer with all of his grotesque depictions carries the weight and blame of every sin imaginable and is not only goatlike, but in many ways he is humanity's ultimate scapegoat who embodies the worst qualities and proclivities that humanity has to offer." The Creator's voice reverberated a little louder. "You cannot have the light without the dark. They are complementary, and each one enhances the other, so much of the history and mythology of Satan the

Prince of Darkness has been told in his role as the counterpart to the stories and mythologies of Jesus the Prince of Peace, who is credited as saying, 'I am the light of the world. Whoever follows me will never walk in darkness, but will have the light of life.'

"I find it fascinating that Jesus the light bearer who represents all things good in humanity and Satan the Prince of Darkness who represents the bad are two of humanity's greatest scapegoats. Apparently the light and the dark are equally deserving of bearing the sins of humanity which begs the question, in the eyes of humanity is there really any difference between Jesus and Satan? Satan after all is Lucifer, an angel who was cast from Heaven into Hell because he rebelled against God. Lucifer means bearer of light or morning star, and refers to his former splendor as the greatest of the angels. This paradox indicates that in the eyes of humanity the light and the dark are one and the same, something one might call a greater Cosmic truth. If you can't accept that then you have to accept the fact of the Great Mystery that *I Am*, that underlies it."

"The myth of my life is a lot shorter than Lucifer's," Jesus said, "but it has endured for almost as long and it has its own inventiveness, confusion, and scapegoating. I was a first-century Jewish religious leader who became *the* central figure of Christianity. Most Christians believe that I was the incarnation of God the Son and the Messiah prophesied in the Old Testament."

Lucifer sparkled. "My twin bearer of the light for humanity and emissary of the light of Heaven."

All three of them glowed brighter before Jesus continued.

"I debated fellow Jews on how to best follow God and did healings, taught in parables, and gathered followers until I was arrested and tried by the Jewish authorities, turned over to the Roman government, and crucified. After my death my followers believed that I rose from the dead and the community they formed became the early Church. Christians believe that I performed miracles, founded the Church, died as a sacrifice to achieve atonement, rose from the dead, and ascended into Heaven with a promise to return one day. Most Christians believe that I enable people to be reconciled to God. The Nicene Creed asserts that I will judge the living and the dead either before or after their bodily resurrection, and most Christians worship me as the incarnation of God the Son."

"I find it endlessly amusing," the Creator's voice echoed, "that as an emissary of my light, you are worshipped as *My* incarnation, while Lucifer your equal light bringer, the morning star and bringer of the dawn no less, has been vilified, demonized, and described in the most derogatory manner."

"Just doing my part as the opposite pole," Satan joked.

The heavens rumbled and the brightness flickered with their combined laughter.

"Christians designated *me* as the Christ," Jesus continued, "because they believed that I was the Messiah whose arrival was prophesied in the Hebrew Bible and Old Testament and in time *Christ* became viewed as a name, one part of Jesus Christ. The four gospels of the New Testament emphasize my different aspects. In Mark, I am the Son of God whose mighty works demonstrate the presence of God's Kingdom. I am portrayed as a tireless wonder worker and the servant of both God and man.

"The Gospel of Matthew emphasizes that I am the fulfillment of God's will as revealed in the Old Testament, Lord of the Church, and the Son of David, a king, *and* the Messiah.

"Luke presented me as a divine-human savior who shows compassion to the needy, and the friend of sinners and outcasts who came to seek and save the lost. Sorry Lucifer, I don't mean to poach from your kingdom."

Satan suppressed a giggle. "No offense taken, brother. All paths do lead to Rome, right?"

"I guess it did for me," Jesus said, but in my case, I'm not so sure that it was the greatest destination. Anyway, the Gospel of John identifies me as an incarnation of the divine Word eternally present with God, active in all creation, and the source of humanity's moral and spiritual nature. I was not only considered greater than any past human prophet, but greater than any prophet could be. I not only spoke God's Word; I *was* God's Word. In the Gospel of John I revealed my divine role publicly as the Bread of Life, the Light of the World, the True Vine, and more. According to the scriptures when John the Baptist baptized me, when I came out of the water he saw the Holy Spirit descending to me like a dove and heard a voice from Heaven declaring me to be God's Son."

"What a great beginning," Satan said. "Beats being thrown out of heaven!"

"Good point," Jesus said, "and I have to say, kudos to you for your part in this story for making me look so good."

"My pleasure!"

"As the story goes, the holy spirit drove me into the wilderness where I was tempted by Satan before I began my ministry after John's arrest. Matthew also detailed my baptism and the three temptations Satan offered me in the wilderness. In Luke, the Holy Spirit descends as a dove after everyone has been baptized and I am praying. John recognized me from prison after sending his followers to ask about me, and my baptism and temptation served as preparation for my ministry.

"The first took place north of Judea, in Galilee, where I conducted a successful ministry and in the second I was rejected and killed when I travelled to Jerusalem. The Galilean ministry began when I returned from the Judaean Desert after rebuffing the temptation of Satan. When I preached around Galilee I appointed twelve apostles and my first disciples formed the core of the early Church. This period included the Sermon on the Mount, one of my major discourses as well as the calming of the storm, the feeding of the five-thousand, walking on water, and a number of other miracles and parables. It ends with the Confession of Peter and the Transfiguration. I taught in parables about the Kingdom of God which was described as both imminent and already present, and promised inclusion for those who accepted his message and talked of the Son of Man, an apocalyptic figure who would come to gather the chosen. I called people to repent their sins and devote themselves to God. When asked what the greatest commandment was, I told them, you shall love the Lord your God with all your heart, and with all your soul, and with all your mind. My second was, you shall love your neighbor as yourself.

"Other teachings included loving your enemies, refraining from hatred and lust, turning the other cheek, and forgiving people who sinned against you. I also said my teaching is not mine but his who sent me. And I asked, do you not believe that I am in the Father and the Father is in me? The words that I say to you I do not speak on my own; but the Father who dwells in me does his works."

"I couldn't have said it better," the Creator added.

"In gospel accounts I devoted a large portion of my ministry performing healing miracles that included cures for physical ailments, exorcisms, and resurrections of the dead. Nature miracles showed my power over nature including turning water into wine, walking on water, and calming a storm, among others. I told them that my miracles were from a divine source and when I was accused of performing exorcisms by the power of Beelzebub, the prince of demons, I countered that I performed them by the Spirit or finger of God."

"And in their blinded ignorance, none of them saw the truth hidden within it all," the Creator said. "It did not matter whether it was the power of you *or* Lucifer. Both of you are expressions of my all inclusive light, loved equally by me in every way."

Satan brightened.

"A major part of this story was the Transfiguration," Jesus said, "when I took Peter and two other apostles up a mountain, where I was transfigured before them, my face shone like the sun, and my clothes became dazzling white. A bright cloud appeared around them, and a voice from the cloud said, 'This is my Son, the Beloved; with him I am well pleased; listen to him'.

"The description of the last week of my life occupies about a third of the whole narrative in the canonical gospels starting with my triumphant entry into Jerusalem and ending with my crucifixion. In this account when I rode a young donkey into Jerusalem people laid cloaks and palm fronds in front of me and sang. I expelled money changers from a temple, accusing them of turning it into a den of thieves, then I prophesied about the coming destruction, including false prophets, wars, earthquakes, celestial disorders, persecution of the faithful, the appearance of an abomination of desolation, and unendurable tribulations. I said the mysterious Son of Man would dispatch angels to gather the faithful from all parts of the earth."

"Great job on your prophesies!" Satan said. "More than two thousand years after you spoke them they have endured and become even more relevant in the twentieth and twenty first centuries."

Jesus snickered. "Thank you for the credit, but we both know that it wasn't really me. It was the Creator speaking through me."

The radiance from the Source glowed brighter followed by the lights of Jesus and Satan until their combined light merged into the Source.

"And of course I came into conflict with the Jewish elders when they questioned my authority," Jesus said, "and I criticized them and called them hypocrites, then Judas betrayed me for thirty silver coins. The Last Supper is the final meal that I shared with my apostles in Jerusalem before my crucifixion where I predicted that one of them would betray me, and despite each apostle's assertion that they would not, I knew Judas was the traitor.

"In the Last Supper I broke bread and gave it to my disciples, saying, this is my body, which is given for you. I told them all to drink wine from a cup, saying, this cup that is poured out for you is the new covenant in my blood. The Christian sacrament is based on this event. I also predicted that Peter would deny knowledge of me three times before the rooster crowed the next morning. We all went to the garden of Gethsemane where I prayed to be spared my coming ordeal, then Judas came with an armed mob and kissed me to show me to the crowd who arrested me. After my arrest my disciples went into hiding, and like I predicted, Peter, denied knowing me three times. After the third denial he heard the rooster crow and recalled my prediction about his denial.

"I was taken to a Jewish judicial body, then to the high priest, Caiaphas, where I was mocked and beaten. During the trials I mounted no defense and gave indirect answers to the priest's questions, prompting an officer to slap me. My unresponsiveness led Caiaphas to ask, 'Have you no answer? Are you the Messiah, the Son of the Blessed One?' I said, 'I am', and then I predicted the coming of the Son of Man provoking Caiaphas to tear his robe in anger and accuse me of blasphemy.

"The Jewish elders took me to ask the Roman governor, Pontius Pilate, to judge and condemn me, accusing me of claiming to be the King of the Jews and Pilate sent me to Herod to be tried. Herod and his soldiers made fun of me, put an expensive robe on me to make me look like a king, and returned me to Pilate who called together the Jewish elders and announced that he had not found me guilty. Observing a Passover custom of the time, Pilate allowed one prisoner chosen by the crowd to be released and they chose a murderer named Barabbas. Pilate wrote a sign in Hebrew, Latin, and Greek that read 'Jesus of Nazareth, the King of the Jews', to be affixed to my cross, then he scourged me and sent me to be crucified. The soldiers placed a Crown of Thorns on my head and ridiculed me as the King of the Jews and beat and taunted me, then I was led to Calvary carrying my cross where the soldiers crucified me and cast lots for my clothes while soldiers and passersby laughed at me. One soldier pierced my side with a lance, and blood and water flowed out and when I died the heavy curtain at the Temple was torn and an earthquake broke open tombs.

"I had to make a little statement," the Creator said, as if apologizing.

"Joseph of Arimathea removed my body from the cross, wrapped me in a clean cloth and buried me in a new rock-hewn tomb. On the following day the chief Jewish priests asked Pilate for the tomb to be secured and with his permission the priests placed seals on the large stone covering the entrance. In Matthew's account Mary Magdalene went to the tomb on Sunday morning and found it empty, then an angel descended from Heaven, opened the tomb, and the guards fainted from fear. I appeared to Mary Magdalene and the eleven remaining disciples in Galilee and commissioned them to baptize all nations in the name of the Father, Son, and Holy Spirit.

"In Mark, a young man in a white robe who is an angel told them that I would meet my disciples in Galilee. In Luke, Mary and other women met two angels at the tomb, but the eleven disciples didn't believe their story. I also appeared to two of my followers and to Peter, then appeared that same day to my disciples in Jerusalem. Although I appeared and vanished mysteriously, I ate and let them touch me to prove that I was not a spirit. In John, Mary was alone until Peter came and saw the tomb, then I appeared to her at the tomb and later appeared to my disciples and breathed on them, giving them the power to forgive and retain sins.

"In a second visit to my disciples I proved to a doubting disciple remembered as Doubting Thomas that I was flesh and blood. The disciples returned to Galilee where I made another appearance and performed a miracle known as the catch of one-hundred-fifty-three fish at the Sea of Galilee before I encouraged Peter to serve his followers. My ascension into Heaven was forty days after the Resurrection. As my disciples looked on I was lifted up and a cloud took me out of their sight.

"The Acts of the Apostles described several appearances of me after my ascension. In Acts, Stephen gazed into Heaven and saw me standing at the right hand of God. Just before his death, and on the road to Damascus, the Apostle Paul was converted to Christianity after seeing a blinding light and hearing my voice saying, 'I am Jesus, whom you are persecuting.' After his conversion Paul claimed the title of Apostle to the Gentiles. His influence on Christian thinking turned out to be more significant than any other New Testament author and by the end of the first century, Christianity was recognized as a separate religion from Judaism."

"Jesus is the central figure of Christianity," the Creator said matter of factly, "and Christians believe that through his sacrificial death and resurrection, humans can be reconciled with Me and offered salvation and the promise of eternal life. These doctrines refer to Jesus as the Lamb of God, who should have really been called the scapegoat of humanity who was crucified to fulfill his role as My servant. Jesus is seen as the new and last Adam whose obedience contrasts with Adam's disobedience.

"Christians view Jesus as a role model and believers are encouraged to imitate his God-focused life. That's not such a bad thing. Most Christians believe that Jesus was both human and the Son of God.

Some early beliefs viewed him as subordinate to the Father and others considered him an aspect of Me rather than a separate person. Some truth slipped in here! The Catholic Church resolved the issue by establishing the Holy Trinity, with Jesus both fully human and fully God.

"Trinitarian Christians believe that Jesus is the Logos, God's incarnation and God the Son, both fully divine and fully human, but the doctrine of the Trinity is not universally accepted among Christians. Christians revere not only Jesus, but his name too. Devotions to the Holy Name of Jesus go back to the earliest days of Christianity."

"We both got a bad rap in the end," Satan said, "but at least they acknowledged your connection to the Source."

"It's nice that they recognized that in me, but just like giving me credit for the prophesies that did not originate from me, but came from the Source far beyond me, I feel uncomfortable with them revering me that way."

The Creator spoke up again. "The myths and legends of you and Satan put you in the realm of supernatural deities who hold great fascination and devotion from many humans. You both served the role of being targets of love, hate, fear, and other things both desirable and undesirable from humans.

"You are both credited with being light bearers. Jesus was the light of the world, and Satan was Lucifer, the bearer of light. Aside from being two of humanity's most well known scapegoats who opposed each other in legendary struggles in the name of good and evil, the one thing you have in common is that you are both light bearers. What does that say about the human race when the stories of the ones who bring the light to humanity are persecuted and banished?"

"They love the darkness," Satan said.

"Does that make them Christian or Satanic?" Jesus asked.

"If they love Jesus and are devoted to the light of the world are they any different than those devoted to Satan who is also the bearer of light? For that matter, how many people have been killed in the name of Jesus or *Me* for that matter in war, sacrifices, and other nefarious ways? *I* am the one inescapable constant in all of life, and the imagination of humans have conjured up all manner of supernatural beings, deities, and entities who influence them and dictate what to expect when it's time to come home to Me. How do those versions of what is thought of as real fit in with the greater reality that *I* am?"

"It is a bit of a paradox, isn't it?" Satan said.

Jesus added. "And transcendence comes from its resolution which arises when the two polarities are recognized as two facets of one and the same Source, does it not?"

"In the eyes of much of humanity," the Creator said, "particularly Christians, you are my two opposing energies of good and evil, but in truth you are two facets of my one loving presence. The concept of the morning star is not the only concept applied to both of you. In Revelation Jesus is referred to as the Lion of the tribe of Judah. In Peter Satan is compared to a lion, seeking someone to devour. Jesus is similar to a lion in that he is crowned a king who is royal and majestic. Satan is similar to a lion in that he seeks to devour other creatures. That is where the similarities between Jesus, Satan, and lions end.

"A bright morning star is a star that outshines all the others. Lucifer was a morning star while Jesus, thought of as God incarnate, the Lord of the universe, is the *bright* morning star. Jesus is credited with being the most holy and powerful light in all the universe, so, while both of you are described as morning stars in no sense does this equate Jesus and Satan. Satan is a created being. His light is said to only exists to the extent that I created it. Jesus is called the light of the world in John. Only the light of Jesus is bright and self-existent. Lucifer may be given credit as a morning star, but according to the scriptures he is only a poor imitation of the one true bright morning star, Jesus Christ, the light of the world.

"Lucifer, you have been loyal to a most sacred task." The Creator glowed brighter. "You have been a scapegoat for bad things that people say that you did including satanic rituals and all the other sins attributed to you. All any human needs to enter into what they think of as heaven is to embrace the light of truth which you two are the two poles of that I have manifested," the Creator said.

Lucifer's glow increased and Jesus followed.

"My, or I should say *our* all-encompassing light shines in order to make My truth accessible no matter where and in what degree of light or darkness any of my human creations stand in, for the only way to enter into and find their way home to me is to embrace the light of truth that *I* Am, but in their fear based ignorance that keeps them in the dark, most of humanity chooses the path of fear and has made you, my two bearers of light, their scapegoats each in their own unique ways to project their sins onto so they do not have to look at or take responsibility for themselves or their actions."

The glow of their essences merged into a light so bright its brilliance would blind anyone not pure enough to withstand it, and the

Creator's voice reverberated from the Source through all of them simultaneously.

"I live in the hearts of men and bear witness to their truths, foibles, and decisions, as well as what they act upon and how important real truth is to them. This allows me to see where and how they lead themselves into darkness. So many humans have wondered how I could be omniscient and allow so much darkness to run rampant on the earth, and how I could let the evil Satan have his way with so much death and destruction, although I would argue that more death, destruction, and torture has been committed in the name of Jesus or simply in My name alone by the folly of invoking my power with prayer, falsely thinking that because my omniscience has been called upon that I will favor and intercede for the supplicant simply because they asked. The greater reality is that each individual is responsible for the consequences of their actions, yet they scatter before the light which only makes it brighter in the same way that blowing on coals stokes a fire.

"Ultimately the light and the dark are one and the same dictated by individual choices, and the only way any being can bear witness to the light of my presence is by embracing the awesome light of truth that I am. The last two lines of Ode on a Grecian Urn written by the English poet John Keats captures the essence of the Great Mystery that we are the faces of.

"'Beauty is truth, truth beauty, — that is all Ye know on earth, and all ye need to know.'"

The combined light of divinity flashed into a dazzling supernova whose brilliance exceeded anything remotely perceptible to any intelligence seen or unseen within the known and unknown reaches of all creation.

MATTHEW J. PALLAMARY

LET US PRAY

His perceptions blazed prismatic with vivid colors, movement, and details, all holding him spellbound like dazzling gems reflecting intense colors and hues. The impact of his exquisite living tapestry and the depth of its detail rearranged his senses in unimaginable ways.

The world around him buzzed, chirped, chittered, rustled, whispered, and vibrated, coming to him in crystal clear, yet inexplicable ways. He did not hear this symphony from both sides of himself in any way he recognized. What he "heard" he felt as one and the same vibration at the center of his abdomen. The sound itself sounded weak, but what it lacked in auditory energy was enhanced by the fluttering sensation he felt more than saw.

Though a mystery in and of themselves, their uniqueness paled in comparison to the rich visual tableau they immersed him in. He continued paying attention, exploring the differing pathways that brought these incredible puzzling perceptions. A fluttering breeze brought him unexpected information in the form of two antennae that extended from his head bringing their own unique vibrations to his feeling-hearing sense, and on the quivering breeze came the scents of life that drove his hunger.

His added sensations and heightened awareness led to the realization that along with his antennae he had six legs, and his head was triangular with bulging eyes. Three small eyes in the middle of his head showed him light while his bigger compound eyes brought movement and depth of vision. His neck felt oddly fluid.

Like Kafka's Gregor Samsa, Jason thought, *only I'm not a cockroach, I'm a Praying Mantis! My God. What a blessing. No wonder everything looks and feels so surreal and amazing!*

The fluttering came closer, becoming a rapid flapping hum and his head turned on instinct in a full half circle to look directly behind him where he was dazzled by the flurry of bright iridescent multicolored flashes from beating wings and a fluid, darting body dancing in the air beneath them.

It hovered and darted off. He snapped his head back forward and the hummingbird returned, hovering over him, before circling around to face him. He remained unmoving, his four back legs locked on the branch beneath him. The buzz of the wings ceased as the bird perched on the branch in front of him, sending him into a sensory overload of sights, smells, and energies. His forelegs erupted like the cracking of a whip and in one continuous motion his claws struck and pierced both sides of the bird's feathered head with lightning speed, embracing it and sinking his mandibles through its skull to suck out the quivering pink fatty morsel inside it.

His explosive gratification drove him awake, wide-eyed and smiling.

"What a blessing!" he whispered, replaying the dream in his mind, savoring every detail.

Entomologist Jason Chen Phd. sat up and swung his legs over the side of the bed, staring at himself in the mirror. Lanky and angular, his awkward mannerisms contrasted his brilliant mind. He rubbed his half-open eyes, and stared at his thin face, narrow pointed nose, and close cropped black hair and frowned.

Gregor Samsa, he thought and giggled feeling giddy.

He stepped into his office at Mantis Optical Labs later that morning and studied the job posting and the list of candidates scheduled to be interviewed that day, both dreading and hoping for the right person. He felt uncomfortable with this part of the process, as his social skills were awkward, but he knew it was a necessary evil needed to move the project forward.

Entomology lab assistant required for research project. A doctoral degree in entomology, biology or zoology is desired, or equivalent experience with a focus on earth science, chemistry, biology, botany, and mathematics.

He left the papers on his desk and went into the lab to put himself in the right frame of mind for the task ahead and stood before his altar to offer his prayers.

Small plant filled terrariums lined one wall each holding a different species of praying mantis. Some looked like leaves, others branches, or flowers. Most were green, but some had brownish tones and colors that camouflaged them in their environments. A lab bench covered in colorful woven and embroidered cloths with assorted stone, clay, shell, wood and bone praying mantis effigies circled the perimeter. In its center sat little bamboo cages containing his prize specimens of mantises that mimicked flowers with colorations and patterns that lured prey. At the very center a little golden cage held an orchid mantis with brilliant coloring and a structure that closely mimicked parts of the orchid flowers it hid in.

Starting at the top terrarium and working his way down, Jason fed each mantis a cricket, saying good morning to each one, ending at his prized orchid mantis, then he knelt down on a padded kneeling bench before the altar, bowed his head, and silently prayed.

I give this nourishment as an offering of gratitude for all you have given me and I open myself to all that I might receive, and ask in all humility that you bring me an assistant who understands me and contributes to the work I do here.

I accept that we are one and the same in spirit, and only wish to serve in the greatest way possible so that I can be of service, deserving of the honor your gracious and honorable spirit requires.

He spent most of the day interviewing male and female applicants, some with lab experience and some with a bachelor's degrees in entomology with a broad education in biological and physical sciences. None of them showed any particular interest in praying mantises, but that was not a requirement for the job. An entomology degree with sufficient lab experience would fit the bill. Toward the latter part of the day he found what he thought to be the answer to his prayers in René Jenkins, an insect enthusiast with an analytical mind and well-rounded laboratory experience. Jason had not shown the lab to any other applicants, but felt compelled to show it to Jenkins, and was impressed with the familiarity of the lab that Jenkins had and his positive comments about what he called the terrarium wall.

Jason had one last interview which he would have cancelled as he was convinced that he had found the perfect assistant in Jenkins, but it was only right that he go through the motions and give the interview.

He looked up from her resume when she came through the door and his breath caught in his chest. He quickly stood and held out his hand. "Jason Chen."

She held out a slender hand adorned with expensive jeweled rings and the delicate scent of jasmine filled his senses.

"Jing Hou-Ghen," she said, but my friends call me by my American name of Patty."

Long, dark silken hair framed green, delicate almond shaped eyes and an elegant string of pearls graced her neck. Her tight fitting teal silk dress accented the curves of her lithe figure. Her regal manner and perfect appearance made him think of royalty and everything about her spoke of wealth.

He struggled for words, finally gesturing to the chair across the desk from his. "Please, have a seat."

She sat with her hands folded demurely in her lap and crossed legs that seemed to go on forever.

Feeling awkward, Jason made a show of picking up and studying her resume. "You have an impressive education, but I don't see any work experience."

"I have been very lucky with my circumstances and haven't had to work, so I have concentrated on furthering my education."

"That's admirable, but why would you want to work here?"

She bowed her head and closed her eyes, then gazed up at him, speaking softly. "I'm a little embarrassed to admit this and I realize that it is not a proper qualification for the job, but I have had a lifelong love of praying mantises."

Jason sat up straight in his chair. "That is an unusual admission. What made you become so interested in them and what is it about them that you find so interesting?"

She put her hands together as if in prayer, bowed her head, and a faraway look came into her eyes followed by the sweetest smile he had ever seen. "I learned from my mother who was a great admirer of their special qualities."

"What special qualities are you referring to?"

Her smile grew. "Since long ago praying mantises have been considered the symbols of truth, peace, and calm, and it is believed that seeing one can be a symbol of good luck."

Is this the answer to my prayers? Jason thought. "Please, go on."

"The first thing that we can relate to a praying mantis is peace and they are also a symbol of mindfulness. In China it has been honored for its amazing mindful movements and its symbolism includes patience, awareness, intuition, and creativity."

Jason's heart beat faster and he realized his palms felt sweaty. He wasn't so sure about Jenkins anymore. *This could really be the answer to my prayers. Someone who understands me.* He stood and leaned in toward Patty, speaking in a confidential tone. "I'm impressed. Perhaps the depth of your knowledge makes up for your lack of lab experience. I'd like to show you something to see what you think?"

She brightened. "Please. I'd be honored.

Jason came around the desk and led her to the lab, opening the door for her and ushering her in.

She stopped two steps in and gasped when she saw his altar, then bowed her head, speaking in a half-whisper. "What a beautiful shrine!"

She glanced at the kneeling bench and looked to Jason, who nodded, then she knelt down, bowed her head, and spoke in tiny whispers, then she rose and studied the specimens on his altar taking turns whispering "Hello", to each of them, then to Jason. "My mother taught me that for praying mantis people, the most important thing is for them to have inner peace. They always think everything through and they never take any action before they are completely sure. That's why they never make mistakes. They are patient and ready to wait until the best opportunity for them comes. It is believed that a praying mantis has the ability to speak to the unknown and to receive messages from it."

Jason couldn't believe what he was hearing. His heart felt like it would explode with love, gratitude, and respect and his whole body tingled with excitement. His prayers were answered in ways he never could have imagined. This was just too good to be true. *Sorry Jenkins*, he thought, *you just got replaced*. "Tell me more," he said, struggling to contain his excitement.

"As I have said, a praying mantis is a symbol of peace and harmony. You will have a peaceful life and you will always know exactly where you are going. If a praying mantis is your spirit animal it will teach you all the benefits that meditation can bring you and calm your mind to live peacefully." She nodded slowly and a tiny smile appeared. "Stillness is another super power of a praying mantis which is part of a peaceful life. It is known that a praying mantis uses stillness to make important decisions and strategies, and with this comes mindfulness." Her smile brightened and she locked eyes with Jason. "Praying mantises are one of the most intelligent insects in the world. They have the ability to hunt other insects and never show fear." She graced him with a full smile. "The praying mantis usually comes to those people who are intelligent, patient, and calm."

Jason felt overwhelmed by Patty, not only for her beauty, but her spirituality. Her esoteric knowledge of praying mantises brought a deeper dimension to his work. He struggled for words feeling speechless, then he found himself talking about his project. He picked up a small tray with rows of tiny 3D glasses with a red lens on one side and blue lens on the other. "Praying mantises are the only invertebrates known to see in 3D, but their depth perception only works when the prey is moving. To dive deeper into their neurobiology we designed miniature 3D glasses to a mantis' face and showed them insect movies." He held the tray up and the tiny red and blue lenses sparkled under the lab lights. "We showed them movies of moving dots that looked like prey camouflaged against a matching background while they wore the glasses. They tried to catch whatever appeared to be within 2.5 centimeters of their perch.

"Humans see in 3D by stitching together the actual image coming in from one eye versus the other, but praying mantises only stitch together motion, regardless of the image. It's the first time this kind of 3D vision has been found in nature. It is our hope that the grant funding our research will help develop robots to navigate the world like the mantises do."

She clasped her hands together like an excited little girl. "How exciting! I would love to work here with you." She lowered her voice. "Honestly, I don't even care about the money. Just being close to your magnificent shrine brings me great happiness."

"If I chose you, I would insist on paying you a fair wage."

She knelt down in front of the altar again, scrunched her eyes shut and prayed in fervent whispers, then stood and faced Jason with an open, sweet, wide-eyed expression. "When will you make your decision?"

Perfect, Jason thought, barely able to contain his excitement. "I already have."

Her expression softened.

He held back for a beat, then asked, "When can you start?"

She bowed low, then rose to full height looking radiant. "Thank you!" she gushed. "First thing Monday morning?"

Jason beamed at the beautiful, angelic answer to his prayers, and felt doubly blessed by the fact that she not only understood his altar, *she had actually prayed at it like he did!* "If you are free, I'd like to treat you to a welcome, get acquainted and congratulations dinner." He held up a finger. "On **Mantis Optical Labs**, of course! I could also fill you in on some of the technical aspects of the project and I'd like to hear more about your mother and how she raised you, but please don't feel any obligation. You may have other plans, and we will have plenty of time to catch up while working together."

"I'd love that," she said. "Thank you! I know I am lacking in my knowledge of laboratory equipment and I am anxious to learn, but I am very good at math and working with computers."

Jason held the door open for Patty, who smiled as she walked past him into Sardina's, his favorite Italian restaurant. All eyes were on Patty as the maitre d' guided them to a reserved candlelit booth at the back.

I need a drink to settle me down, Jason thought, sliding into the booth next to Patty. *I feel like I'm jumping out of my skin.* "If you're okay with it," he said leaning in to her smelling jasmine, "I'd like to order a bottle of Dom Perignon to celebrate properly."

"That sounds lovely." Patty looked up to the maitre d' who smiled and nodded before stepping away, returning a minute later with menus and Dom Perignon in a silver bucket with two champagne glasses, which he filled.

"Here's to you." Jason raised his glass.

"And to you and our project," Patty said, lightly touching her glass to his and taking a sip.

Jason downed his glass and poured himself a second. Warmth filled him and he felt himself relaxing. "My favorite dish here is Shrimp Scampi with Linguini," he said, looking over the top of his menu.

"I was thinking the same thing," Patty said, lowering hers.

They ordered and ate, chatting between bites while Jason outlined how he saw their project unfolding. While pouring his fourth glass of Dom Perignon, he noticed Patty still sipping her first. He felt a little embarrassed, but the warm fuzzy feeling the champagne gave him bathed him inside and out along with the soft glow of sparkling candlelight that made Patty look more angelic than ever.

Her jeweled rings sparkled on slender hands and her earrings and pearls twinkled along with her glistening green eyes and bright teeth against her shimmering black hair like so many stars in the night sky.

Everything flowed and he couldn't help himself from saying, "I don't mean to make you uncomfortable, and please correct me if I am crossing any boundaries that I shouldn't be, but for whatever it is worth, I feel like you are my twin flame." He held his hands out in surrender. "I am not saying this lightly, but I believe that you are the literal answer to my prayers."

He folded his hands in front of him and she rested her hand on his and gave it a gentle squeeze, then she looked into his eyes while the delicate scent of jasmine filled his senses.

He basked in her presence and things became more dreamlike and blurry, then he jolted like he had been awakened from a nap. Patty's adoring gaze stayed on him as he called for the bill and paid it. Once outside he stumbled a little. "Sorry, I got a little carried away with the celebrating."

She giggled and took his hand. "I'm not going to let you drive like that. I'll take you home."

"I can't let you…"

"I insist. We can't risk anything happening to you. It would ruin the whole project."

He sighed. "Well if you put it that way." She giggled again and pulled him along. "Come one, I'll drive you." She led him to a shiny black Tesla and drove him home.

Though he had stopped drinking his fuzziness and the exquisite feelings he felt with Patty increased to the point where she had to help him into his house. Once inside she helped him to his bedroom and stood facing him. Something inside of him surrendered and he kissed her on the lips.

She opened her soft lips and engaged him while hugging him close and he embraced her in return, reveling in her softness and curves, and the intoxicating scent of jasmine.

She turned away and motioned for Jason to pull down the zipper on her dress and he watched, admiring her swaying backside as she wiggled out of her dress.

She helped Jason undress and crawled on top of him. Every cell of his being felt electrified every place her skin touched him, then she mounted him, thrusting hard. His perceptions blazed prismatic with vivid colors that held him spellbound like brilliant animated gems reflecting surreal colors and hues. She pushed harder and cried out while his body spasmed in exquisite pleasure that blossomed from the bottom up into a massive full body orgasm that peaked into a brilliant white flash.

Later that week different versions of the following story filled much of the news cycle throughout the internet.

Authorities have discovered the decapitated body of noted entomologist Jason Chen. Investigators are puzzled over the bizarre crime and are at a loss to explain any clues as to the fate of Chen's missing head.

"We can't explain it," a source close to the investigation said. "There's no trace of anything. It's as if his head got swallowed up out of nowhere."

THE SEVEN DWARFS

Corporate raider Hodge Crabtree pulled his Tesla into an underground parking lot, happy to get it in out of the rain. He checked himself in the mirror to see that his pinstriped Armani suit looked spotless and his red power tie and styled hair were all perfectly in place, then he grabbed his briefcase and umbrella and glanced at his Rolex before walking two blocks to the offices of another company he would soon control.

Ten minutes until the board of director's meeting where he would make his signature move of buying the majority of undervalued shares which would let him install his own people into management positions. This tactic would increase share value before he broke the company up and sold it off in portions for a premium price resulting in a healthy return for him.

He stopped when a clanking sound from the end of a long alley captured his attention, and peered through the falling rain in time to see a short, bald, stumpy looking homeless man with a bushy white beard dressed in ragged clothes climb into a dumpster and pull the lid down over him.

"Disgusting," he muttered, wrinkling his nose.

He tried to shake it, but the image made him think of Grumpy from the Seven Dwarfs disappearing into some kind of subterranean hobbit hole. He shook his head and moved on to the gleaming office building where his two grey suited aggressive young attorneys with matching red ties and short cropped black hair waited with the contracts needed to follow through with the takeover. He referred to Harry Smith and John Weston as his hired guns and addressed them as Smith and Wesson.

A thin, quivering, white haired old man with a bushy mustache dressed in a gray frumpy looking seersucker suit who reminded Hodge of the top-hatted Monopoly man sat on one side of a long table in a small spartan glass walled conference room. His two middle aged sons who looked like younger fitter versions flanked him and two of his own sharply dressed attorneys sat at each end beside them while Hodge and his two man team took up the other side of the table.

He had hoped to complete the action swiftly in his own version of corporate blitzkrieg, but the old man stonewalled the proceedings with his feeble efforts to stop the inevitable causing the meeting to drag on interminably. Hodge kept his cool, but beneath the surface it took every ounce of control he could muster to keep from venting his frustration at the old codger. At the point where he thought he would explode, his lead attorney intervened.

"You have all the documents and all the figures," Hodge's man said, "and we are offering you a very fair deal."

The old man held up his hand. "It's not that simple," he said in a reedy voice. "This business started in a garage and has been in the family for generations, so..."

"Let's cut with the sentiment," Hodge said. "This is business, not family home week. You're books are bleeding red and bankruptcy is just around the corner. If you have any common sense you'll take our offer or we'll withdraw it and buy you out in bankruptcy court."

The old man's eyes grew wide as if he'd been slapped in the face. "But what about our employees, many of them..."

Hodge rose from his chair and gathered up his papers "It's been a long day and I'm not here to quibble over minutiae. We'll leave you with the documents so you can talk it over." He dropped his paperwork into his briefcase and snapped it shut. "You have twenty four hours to accept our offer. Otherwise we'll exercise our options and force you into court and you know what will happen there."

"But..."

"Contact my attorneys when you're ready to sign." He spun on his heels and walked out, leaving them all behind and kept going to the elevator, thinking, *Got him!*

He stepped out into the pouring rain and opened his umbrella, careful to keep it at the right angle so he didn't get his suit or hair wet and strutted down the street feeling self-satisfied.

He looked down to avoid a puddle when he came to the alleyway he had passed earlier, took a tentative step, and glanced up a split second before walking straight into Grumpy who came around the corner lugging two bulging black Hefty Lawn and Leaf bags. Cans and bottles scattered everywhere as Grumpy tumbled to the ground in front of him, landing in the middle of the puddle splashing muddy water all over Hodge's Armani suit and Dolce & Gabbana Crocodile loafers.

"Jesus Christ!" Hodge screamed. "Why don't you watch where you're going you disgusting slob." He looked down at his mud spattered suit and shoes. "Shit! You fucked up my clean suit and shoes."

Grumpy sat in the puddle looking like a drowned rat covered in wet rags staring up at him with a vacant expressionless stare and no emotion. His lack of reaction angered Hodge even more. His rage erupted and he kicked the degenerate, instantly regretting the act when he felt Grumpy's softness which made his skin crawl at the thought of any contact with the vile creature.

Grumpy's expression remained placid and indifferent as if nothing had happened.

"Son of a bitch!" Hodge kicked at the scattered cans and bottles sending them flying in all directions. "Get a life you dumpster diving maggot."

Still no reaction.

Hodge stormed off and looked over his shoulder at the dumpster at the end of the alley and saw five more ragged looking rain-soaked homeless men staring at him through the rain with what looked like blank expressions similar to Grumpy's. *Great,* he thought. *There's five more of the fucking dwarfs. Smelly, Ratty, Dumpy, Sleazy, and Trashfull.*

He quickened his step, anxious to get home and get out of his contaminated suit. His stomach turned at the thought of handling his shoes which had touched the cretin, so he threw them out and took a long hot shower to make sure he didn't catch any germs or diseases, then he called the mobile detailer to come clean and sanitize his car.

The rain stopped that night and the following day began hot and dry. By the time he left for his meeting that afternoon all signs of the previous day's rain had disappeared. He pulled his car into the parking lot, anxious to finish the deal and slowed when he walked up to the alleyway. Sure enough, he saw Grumpy, Smelly, Ratty, Dumpy, Sleazy, and Trashfull swarming around the dumpster like so many rats.

He struggled with his rising disgust and realized he was shaking partially from fear until his anger overcame his revulsion. He stormed down the alley until the sour smelling effluvium of the dumpster combined with the pungent stink of shit and piss stopped him as if repulsed by a solid, palpable wall of stink.

Where's the fucking exterminators when you need one?, he thought. His stomach felt queasy and he wanted to breathe in to calm himself, but he didn't dare. "Get out of the trash you disgusting disease spreading vermin!" he yelled, shaking his fist.

They all stopped and turned to stare at him with the same blank expression that had spooked him so badly the day before. They stood motionless for a small eternity before each one picked up his own bulging black Hefty bag and walked past him in single file led by Grumpy. He stumbled back against the wall as they passed acting as if he didn't exist, carrying the stink with them. He nearly vomited at their stench as they passed.

Hi Ho, Hi Ho, it's off to work we go, he thought feeling giddy. "I'd better not see you back here or I will call the police and have you all forcibly removed!"

He took a few moments to compose himself, then walked to the end of the alley on shaking legs and peered around the corner to insure that they had gone. With no sign of them on the street he hustled to his meeting where he found his smiling attorneys waiting with the signed contracts laid out on the table in front of his seat in the center spot on his side of the conference room. The resigned old man and his sons sat with their heads bowed in silence on the other side of the table.

"You made the right choice." He took his lucky Montblanc Meisterstuck Classique 164 Gold-plated Ballpoint Pen from his pocket. "It's a fair deal and I kept you out of bankruptcy court, so your reputation is secure." He smiled and shuffled through the contracts signing and initialing all of the places highlighted in yellow by his attorneys and looked up to see the old man slowly shaking his head.

Smith and Wesson sorted through the documents as Hodge signed and passed copies across the table to the old man and his sons.

"I hope you take care of our loyal employees and treat them fairly," the old man said in a barely audible voice. "I'm counting on you to do the honorable thing and keep them employed. They have families."

His two sons studied Hodge with accusing stares, reinforcing their father's words.

"I can assure you, we only want what's best for all," Hodge said with mock sincerity. *Which will be pink slips that will put them out of their misery*, he added mentally. He made a show of checking his Rolex. "Now if you'll excuse me we have another pressing engagement."

Hodge snapped his briefcase shut, rose from the table and left the room followed by his attorneys.

"You guys did a great job wrapping that one up," Hodge said once they were in the elevator. "Drinks are on me at La Valencia."

A rose colored sunset bathed the horizon as they left the building and walked the few short blocks to La Valencia where Hodge opened a tab at the bar and ordered a bottle of Dom Perignon. Halfway through the bottle a waiter lined up two shots of bourbon in front of each man.

"What's this?" Hodge blurted out. "I didn't order this!"

"The two best bourbons in the house." Smith raised a shot glass. "One from me and one from Wesson."

Wesson followed suit, raised a glass and downed it. "To show our appreciation to you for giving us the opportunity to structure the amazing deal you just signed off on."

Hodge felt a little tipsy from the champagne and couldn't help but smile. He picked up a shot glass, held it up to Smith, then to Wesson. "To the two best hired guns any man could ever ask for." He held the glass higher and drained it.

Wesson held up the second glass and nodded to Smith to pick up his and Hodge followed. "To the best friend our bank accounts have ever seen!"

They downed the second shot together, smacking them down on the table in unison, then they burst into laughter.

Hodge couldn't remember if they finished the champagne when they left La Valencia, but it didn't matter. When he stepped out onto the darkened street and parted ways with his attorneys he felt like a superhuman king of the world and a conquering hero who had fought his way to the top of the food chain. "Eat your heart out, Alexander," he said under his breath. "Hodge The Great has arrived," he said a little louder as he approached the underground parking lot where his Tesla waited.

The telltale rattling of cans and bottles caught his attention from the end of the darkened alley as if in response to his proclamation.

"What the fu…"

He stopped and peered into the dim light of the alley and spotted six spectral figures carrying Hefty bags moving furtively in the darkness, trooping toward the dumpster at the end of the alley. He lurched forward and fell in at the end of the line behind them, screaming, "What the hell are you vermin doing back here?" He shook his fist. "You malformed maggots are a blight to this beautiful city.

You don't belong here. Go back to whatever shithole you came from!"

The slow march continued, unmoved by his words and actions, and for that matter none of them gave any reaction to anything he did as if he didn't exist. Realizing he had cornered them like rats giving them no means of escape, he stopped in front of the rank smelling dumpster. To his amazement the march continued forward until one by one they disappeared behind the dumpster.

Confusion swept over him and an icy ball of fear settled in the pit of his stomach, then he broke out in a cold sweat and vomited all over himself, splattering puke on his Armani suit and Dolce & Gabbana Crocodile loafers.

His world spun and in that moment of spiraling fear, horror, and disgust, his curiosity rose up causing him to stumble forward. He grabbed the cold, greasy edge of the dumpster to stay on his feet and inched closer to see where they could have possibly gone to. A grimy hand reached out and pulled him in and inexorably down into a blackened foul smelling abyss.

He lost all sense of time and seemed to fall for a never ending eternity until he stopped short, opening his eyes to a small dimly lit cavern with tunnels that went out in multiple directions like so many tentacles. Six sets of feral eyes glinted in the dark like giant rats.

He stood on shaking legs and they circled him, then something sharp and razorlike bit into his ankle. He screamed when another pierced his calf and moved up his leg to the back of his knee sending him sprawling to the ground, then they swarmed over him. Daggers of bright excruciating pain shot through every fiber of his being and his screams intensified, ebbing with each successive bolt of agony until the darkness claimed him.

He came to in the grey light of dawn sitting up against the wall at the back of the alley behind the dumpster covered with bites and oozing sores. He looked down to see his tattered vomit covered suit and shoes slick and shiny with grease and vomit. His wallet and cell phone were gone, but it didn't matter. He couldn't remember who or where he was. He thought about saying something but no words came and that didn't matter either. Speaking didn't seem worth the effort.

The aromas from the dumpster filled his senses and what had previously turned his stomach now smelled intoxicating. He raised his head and looked up into the eyes of Grumpy who smiled down on him with a benevolent grin.

Now they were seven.

FETAL FANTASIES

Jeanette stretched out on the bed, brushed back her long blonde hair, and laid her head on her husband Ted's chest. "If we're going to bring a kid into the world, let's create the most perfect one we can," she said.

Ted leaned in to her. "Like Hitler's blond-haired, blue-eyed Aryan boys?"

Jeanette hit him on the shoulder. "Stop it! I was thinking more along the lines of a Jesus, then again, maybe we want a little girl."

Ted chuckled and kissed her. "I'm okay with a blonde-haired, blue-eyed Jesus, especially if he or she looks like their mother!"

"So many choices." Jeanette sighed. "Part of me wishes we could go back to natural selection like our parents did."

"It's a crap shoot with too many unknowns," Ted said with an air of finality. "Added to that are the worries about birth defects, delivery complications, or other possibilities for trouble, not to mention the threat and the impact to your own health."

"But part of me craves the idea of nurturing a new life inside of me with all the warmth, connection, and intimacy."

Ted caressed the side of her face. "I understand that as best as I can from a man's perspective. I also know that pregnancy can be exhausting, painful, nauseating, and sometimes flat-out dangerous. If you're pregnant and you party, stress too much, get sick or catch some kind of disease, you might not be giving our child the best start we can." He ran his hand down over her breasts and followed her sculpted curves down to the softness of her inner thigh. "Not to mention what it could do to your beautiful body."

She giggled when his hand caressed her thigh. "Stop it!"

He continued his caresses. "Think about the benefits. We can continue having all the sex we want with no interruptions. Aside from that, you might not have the same intensely human birthing experience as your mother had, but we'll both arrive at our first day of parenthood feeling physically fresh and well-rested, instead of you having been weighed down for months by a parasitic organism that tends to leave a path of destruction when you birth it. Even in the best case scenario there are also the possibilities of post-partum depression, hormone imbalances, and other post birth dangers."

"You make it sound so horrible."

"I only want what is best for you and baby. You have to admit, the whole pregnancy thing takes a toll on you. If you take that into consideration and look at the positives, taking advantage of the technological benefits we are blessed with is the best way to go. Everything will be precisely controlled and monitored which eliminates any stress on beautiful *you*, and it ensures the safest, healthiest, most stable environment for our love child to grow in."

They stayed quiet for awhile, then Jeanette sat up and grabbed an iPad from the bed stand. "Let's take another look at it."

She propped herself up against the headboard, pulled her knees up and put the tablet in her lap, tapping the screen. Ted propped himself up beside her and put his arm around her shoulder. A moment later the Fetal Fantasies web site popped up.

Angelic looking baby faces floated up, filling the screen, each framed in baby blue or pink. In the middle of the screen effervescent pulsing pink words dimmed and brightened from a black rectangle along with the gentle throbbing of a tiny heartbeat.

Let Fetal Fantasies eliminate the pain, danger, and discomfort of pregnancy and labor while allowing you the unprecedented blessing of creating your dream child with the special qualities and genetics of your choosing.

Jeanette tapped the pulsing text opening up a new screen.

The Fetal Fantasies Artificial Womb Facility brings a novel approach to pregnancy with the baby growing in an idealized, optimally balanced germ free environment inside a transparent growth pod.

Our proprietary technology replicates ideal gestation conditions in a temperature-controlled, infection-free womb

with a view. An artificial umbilical cord provides oxygen and nutrition as your little bundle of love floats in a pharmaceutically pure amniotic fluid, continually refreshed with precisely tailored hormones, antibodies and growth factors. Baby waste products are efficiently removed and run through a bioreactor which enzymatically converts it back into a steady and sustainable supply of fresh nutrients.

Built in stereophonic speakers ensure that your loved one gets the best possible brain nutrition delivered with binaural beats and direct cranial stimulation, including an ongoing enhanced transmission of your heartbeat that your little one can bond to. As baby grows and develops there are options for our recommended classical, or any other music of your choice as well as your own soothing voice piped in to build and enhance that precious invaluable bond.

A video filled the bottom part of the screen. Jeanette tapped the start arrow and the video opened up into full screen mode.

Brahm's Lullaby played in the background. Technicians dressed in baby blue and pink clean room coveralls, masks, and gloves moved along rows of transparent egg shaped pods sitting atop active graphical displays, stopping to examine each one. Healthy babies floated inside each pod with identical electrodes attached to different parts of their bodies. Clear plastic umbilical cords and other tubes coupled with various monitoring devices hung suspended in clear amniotic fluid. A soothing feminine voice narrated the images and video segments playing out onscreen.

An attractive young couple studied a cell phone screen that matched the graphics on the pod displays.

"You can monitor your baby's vitals through the Fetal Fantasy app or tune directly in to live HD vision in the pod where vital signs are precisely managed allowing strict vigilance over any possible physical defects or genetic abnormalities. Real-time data on your little bundle of love is a few taps away on our phone app along with a live HD fetus cam that gives you the ability to scroll through time-lapse videos of your child's development from embryo to full gestation.

"Human babies are among the most helpless and underdeveloped in the animal kingdom because our brains are too big for the human female hip gap, so we're born undercooked, with soft, pliable skulls, several months behind other animals developmentally, but in a Fetal Fantasy EZ-Womb, there's no such biological limit allowing parents to experiment with longer gestational periods and healthier, more developed babies.

"If this looks and sounds a little impersonal and you think you might miss the feeling of the baby kicking, our haptic suit option can bring that sensation back for any parent that wants it, only when they want it."

An image of the young couple sitting beside each other on a couch wearing VR headsets with wide smiles filled the screen.

"Want to see the beginning of life from your child's point of view? You can with a VR headset that allows you to tune in to a 360-degree camera any time you like."

The image of the young couple panned back showing them in a comfortably furnished room with a large picture window in the background. A baby floated in a single transparent pod above active graphical displays next to a window with an expansive view of a twinkling magical night time cityscape in the background.

"If you're uncomfortable with our standard birth package and are unhappy with the thought of your precious bundle of joy being grown in a 400-pod baby lab, you can have a rechargeable battery-powered pod installed in your own home."

The narration changed to a male announcer's voice. "Fetal Fantasies provides the best option for folks who like the idea of a baby but don't want to go through the ordeals of pregnancy and childbirth to get one. Think about it. You might not even need a day off work! Just hold hands with your significant other after a day at the office, head down to the baby farm and pop the lid on life as a parent, or enjoy your special time in the privacy of your own home."

Alternating pink and blue words dimmed and brightened at the bottom of the screen pulsing in time to the gentle throbbing of a tiny heartbeat.

ENROLL HERE FOR OUR FREE NO OBLIGATION BUILD A BABY WORKSHOP

Ted pulled Jeanette closer. "What do you think, honey?"

"So many choices and options. To be honest, I feel overwhelmed by all of it."

Ted kissed her on the cheek. "We don't have to make any hard decisions now and we have nothing to lose if we try the workshop."

"I still have lots of questions."

"I'm sure they can be answered at the workshop."

Jeanette remained quiet.

"Nothing ventured, nothing gained," Ted whispered.

Jeanette shrugged and tapped the enroll message.

Ted and Jeanette joined half a dozen other couples in the spacious lobby of Fetal Fantasies in a large two story mirrored glass building.

"Welcome to Fetal Fantasies," a statuesque younger woman with expressive hazel eyes, long brown hair, and a form fitting silk teal dress said when they entered. "My name is Harmony, and it's my privilege to take you on a short tour of our facility before we start the workshop."

She gestured toward a mirrored wall that slid open revealing a larger room and waved everybody in.

Floor to ceiling observation windows looked out over a larger room where Brahm's Lullaby played. Technicians in baby blue and pink coveralls moved along row after row of transparent baby pods on top of graphical displays. Babies floated inside each pod with electrodes attached to their bodies and clear plastic umbilical cords and other tubes coupled with monitoring devices hanging suspended in amniotic fluid. A massive video screen hung above it all, cycling through video from the inside of pods, closeup shots, and from other cameras throughout the facility.

Jeanette took Ted's arm and leaned in close, whispering, "It seems so sterile and impersonal."

A moving observation walkway encircled the glass walled enclosure allowing visitors to view the facility from every perspective. Harmony guided them onto it while a pre-recorded male voice spoke from hidden speakers as the group moved around the perimeter, gazing down at the baby farm.

"We are living in a moment of super-convergence of a number of technologies happening at the same time that all influence each other. Affordable sequencing of the human genome allows population-wide phenotypical research to be cross-checked to learn more about how genes express themselves, individually and in concert with one another.

"Artificial intelligence and quantum computing allows us to process monstrous amounts of data, and its capabilities are rocketing forward daily while gene editing tools give us the ability to edit the genome of living subjects. Our highly trained health care professionals facilitate a more personal and precise approach to customize opportunities for people with certain genetic markers.

"Advanced embryo selection is at the core of our IVF treatment. Prospective parents will have multiple embryos to choose from, each of which will have its genome fully sequenced so they can choose between offspring from a large database of information. Parents can select against crippling genetic diseases like Down syndrome guaranteeing them a healthy, happy child.

"Following our proprietary process, new parents can select *for* certain traits as well as against others. Do you want your child to be taller? More athletic, with a greater proportion of fast twitch muscle fibers? What about intelligence? Skin color? Eye color? Would you like to select the genetics for a child with a higher probability of living longer, a child with a higher degree of extraversion, or a more even temperament?

"All of these traits have genetic underpinnings which allows parents to choose between dozens of their own biological embryos, so why wouldn't you choose the one that has the best possible shot at life?

"The disadvantages of having children the old-fashioned way has now become apparent, as smarter, stronger, faster, healthier kids born from selection processes can dominate a range of competitive situations, from sport to business to earning capacity. These advantages will multiply with subsequent generations, as more and more science is applied to the reproductive process.

"Precision gene editing lets you select multiple options from your pre-implanted embryos, and allows you to make a number of adjustments before you implant it.

"The dawn of a new age of superhumans is upon us where a new selected and edited generation will have extraordinary genetic potentials in a wide range of areas."

The moving walkway stopped, allowing everyone to step off. Harmony led them to a classroom where a large flat screen took up one wall with a podium off to its right. Coffee and other refreshments filled a table at the other end of the room. A semi-circle of large desks with chairs for two at each one surrounded the big screen. Each desk had a computer monitor at its center displaying a QR Code onscreen. Ted and Jeanette found their way to a desk and Harmony went to the podium where she pointed to the QR Code up on the big screen. "You can scan the QR Code on your desk monitors with your cell phone to download the Fetal Fantasies app which will synch to your account here, giving you real time access to all of your information, regardless of your location."

Ted and Jeanette scanned the code and downloaded the app along with the other couples. After a moment the screens on their phones matched the display on the big screen and the desk monitor.

"You can make your selections on your phones and they will be displayed on your shared desk monitor," Harmony said.

Every screen had a matching graphic display featuring a spot for baby's name at the top, and the image of a human body at the top right quadrant of the screen. Beside it were two rows of menu buttons labeled with selections like sex, eye color, hair color, vocal timbre, physical build, intelligence factor, athletic requirements, and other features. Below that dimmed out across the bottom of the screen were graphs for heartbeat, respiration, blood pressure, EKG activity, immune development, and other factors.

"Each menu button on your left has a number of submenus for more detailed selections." Harmony pointed a remote at the big screen beside her and demonstrated the menu system by hitting a few buttons, showing more detailed choices. "Take your time and build your love child the way you dreamed of them. Changes are possible up to the moment of conception, and many can be reprogrammed up to the end of the first trimester."

"So many choices," Jeanette said. It feels like too many. It makes me feel like I'm playing God."

"Goddess." Ted set down his phone and rested his hand on hers. "I feel the same way, but I'm excited about the possibilities. Right now it's just a workshop. We have no commitment. Think of it like taking a new car for a test ride at a dealership."

Jeanette rolled her eyes. "That certainly sounds warm and inviting. I can't help thinking that all of this technology separates us from a nurturing intimate flesh and blood connection between baby and mother."

"While you're making your selections," Harmony said, "I will come around to each of you to assist you, and answer any questions. Happy baby making!"

Ted gave Jeanette's hand a gentle squeeze. "Let's see what kind of angelic love child we can create when we put our minds to it." He kissed her cheek. "Don't forget, we can change whatever we want, wipe it all clean and forget about it, or start all over again fresh."

Jeanette brightened "All right. Let's make an angel."

"Even though I want a boy," Ted said, "I know you want a girl. I could do a lot worse to have two blonde-haired, blue-eyed beauties in my life."

"I do want a girl," Jeanette said, "but if we did follow up on this, starting with a boy would give our little girl a big brother to watch over and protect her." She smiled. "Besides, we can change it if we decide differently later." She tapped a menu button on her phone and selected male. The display on their monitor and their cell phones turned blue.

"Let's stick with the blond hair and blue eyes for now," Ted said.

"Sure!" Jeanette hit two more buttons, changing all the displays.

More selections of physical characteristics brought greater detail to the body at the top right of the screens and Jeanette grew more enthusiastic as they selected other attributes. "I'm still not saying I am ready to commit to this," she said, "but if we do, I want to make the most perfect baby possible."

"Of course!"

Harmony joined them at their desk. "How is it going, you two? Any questions?"

"So far, so good," Ted winked. "We're having fun, but Jeanette has more questions."

"The ladies always do. That's what I'm here for."

"I have to admit to being fascinated with all of it," Jeanette said, "but I'm still a little uneasy. This makes me feel like I'm playing God and I can't help thinking how this technology separates us from a warm intimate flesh and blood connection between baby and mother."

"Excellent question," Harmony said. "You are looking at a state of the art baby farm, so I can understand how it comes across as impersonal. This is what you get with our standard birth package. If you're uncomfortable with the thought of your precious bundle of joy being grown in a lab at a baby farm, you can have a rechargeable battery-powered pod installed in your home. Our deluxe package includes a haptic suit option so you can experience all the mommy feelings you might not want to miss out on at your own chosen times and discretion."

Ted studied Jeanette with an expectant look.

"What about breastfeeding?" Jeanette said. "That's one of the primary bonding experiences between mother and child."

Harmony smiled, showing perfect teeth behind plump lips. "We have options there too. We can supply you with our proprietary nutrient dense formula complete with oxytocin and other supportive hormones. We also have a program that combines special supplements and hormonal injections that allow the mother to have the more visceral experience and physical closeness of breastfeeding their child."

"Think of it," Ted added. "You can avoid the pain and discomfort of pregnancy and the wear and tear on that beautiful body of yours and have the ability to experience those feelings when you want instead of all the time. We can work and play to our hearts desire until the day our baby is born."

Harmony held up a finger. "And you will avoid post-partum depression and any other post birth complications. You will be able to embrace and nurture your new born in a fully healthy state."

"That's a lot to think about," Jeanette said.

"Yes, it is," Harmony said, "so there is no pressure and no time limits. Take all the time you need to decide what is right for you. We're here for any questions or assistance you might need. In the mean time, have some fun." She gestured toward their monitor. "It looks like you already have a special child in the making. Call if you need me."

Harmony stepped away and Ted and Jeanette quickly found themselves consumed in creating their dream child.

Three months later a tiny baby floated in a single transparent pod above active graphical displays in a rechargeable battery-powered pod in a darkened corner of Ted and Jeanette's bedroom wirelessly connected to the Fetal Fantasies baby farm network. Ted and Jeanette's cell phones and their respective computers all matched the real time readings on the front panel of the unit's display.

Inside the transparent womb an infant floated in amniotic bliss with fully formed arms, hands, fingers, feet, and toes. The beginnings of fingernails and toenails were visible and its ears were fully formed. A clear plastic umbilical cord and other tubes attached to the infant coupled with monitoring devices suspended in the clear amniotic fluid.

Ted and Jeanette cuddled together in the semi-darkness of their room while the pod pulsed softly in the shadowed corner with the faint sound of a muted heartbeat accompanied by the pulsing red glow of vital signs from the unit's display.

"The sound of his tiny heart and the red glow that goes with it makes me feel like I'm in the womb with him," Jeanette said.

Ted squeezed her a little tighter. "We are the womb, honey! Think about it. A see through womb and the sound of that little beating heart and flashing red connects us and makes us part of it every step of the way."

"That's a nice way to think of it."

"And we can both communicate with him whenever we want, or play him music from anywhere we want just by picking up the phone."

"I'm naming him Theodore after you Ted. We can call him Theo so there's no confusion between the two of you when he gets older."

Over the next few months Theo's heartbeat grew stronger, filling the room in concert with the red pulsing unit. His fingers and toes now looked well-defined and his eyelids, eyebrows, eyelashes, nails, and hair were all visible. His teeth and bones had grown denser, his tiny penis had fully formed, and he had begun to move around.

"Look!" Jeanette said one day, standing in front of the pod. "He's yawning, sucking his thumb, stretching, and making faces. How adorable!"

Ted came closer and put his arm around her, peering into the pod. Theo looked red and wrinkled like a wizened old man and his veins were visible through translucent skin. "Isn't this great. We get to watch his whole development. We wouldn't get to see any of this if he were inside of you."

Theo moved more in the coming weeks and responded to sounds they made when they were in the room as well as changes to the room's light. Ted and Jeanette took turns talking to him through their phones, giggling when they saw him responding to the pod's built in stereophonic speakers.

"He needs some culture," Ted said one day.

"What do you mean?"

He tapped on his phone screen until Pink Floyd's Dark Side of the Moon played through the pod speakers. Theo froze and turned his head to the side as if listening while rocking back and forth with the opening sound of a heartbeat, then looked up when the rest of the music followed. As the album progressed, his movements grew more refined while he moved to the beat in a graceful, flowing weightless ballet.

"Quick," Ted whispered. "Put on the haptic suit and lie down on the bed. I'm dying to see how it works and what you feel."

Jeanette put on the suit while the album continued, activated it and stretched out on the bed. A moment later her body moved in parallel with Theo's as if she were attached to him with strings and he was the puppeteer. "I'm dancing with him," she cried. "I'm dancing with my baby!"

"You're feeling what he's feeling with him. It connects you!"

Ted slid into the bed beside her and held her gently. "Now we're all dancing." Ted reached up from behind and caressed her enlarged breasts. "Those hormones they have been giving you are working great! Your tatas are looking and feeling very nice!"

She slapped his hand away and giggled, "Stop it! These aren't for you. I have no physical connection with Theo and I am looking forward to breast feeding him to seal that intimate mother son bond."

"Well I'm hoping he will be willing to share them at some point. I was here first after all."

Every day they tried something different. When they played classical music, Theo didn't move much and appeared to yawn more, but he always rocked out to Pink Floyd and went into what looked like a trance when they played meditative music from Jeanette's yoga class.

"Everything is so flawless," Jeanette said one day. "He's perfectly formed." She held up her phone to Ted.

"The Fetal Fantasy engineers said that our choices of characteristics and attributes in Theo's genetic profile put him in the highest one tenth of a percentile range of anything they had ever seen."

"We're getting close to his birthday," Jeanette said. "We need to pick what day we want that to be."

Ted kissed her on the cheek. "I can't wait."

Ted jolted awake to Jeanette's screams in the dark.

"What's wrong?"

She looked at him wide-eyed and Ted realized there were no sounds, no lights, and no signs of life. He reached for his cell phone and saw a blank screen, then Jeanette stumbled across the room. "God, please," she whispered.

Ted jumped out of bed and joined her beside the darkened pod where little Theo floated without movement or any signs of life.

"Please god." Jeanette dropped to her knees, clasped her hands together and started whispering prayers. Ted remained dumbfounded a moment before he dropped down beside her and followed suit.

"Dear God," Jeanette said. "Please save our little Theo. I promise to do anything you ask and promise to serve you with all my heart and soul."

The lights in the room flickered on and off and jumbled graphics danced across the pod's display, then the unit thumped to life and the pod pulsed softly with the sound of a muted heartbeat and the pulsing red glow of vital signs from the unit's display showing normal healthy readings.

Ted and Jeanette leaned in close to Theo's pod and watched him yawn and stretch, then to their amazement his eyelids fluttered open wide. Two big bright blue eyes stared back from his wizened wrinkled face taking in Ted and Jeanette with a gaze that seemed to look right through them.

"Wow," Ted said. "Talk about feeling watched. You and I are going to have to start behaving."

She hugged Ted around the waist. "I'm so glad he's safe. What the hell just happened?"

"We need to check in with Fetal Fantasies to find out. Let me see if our phones are working."

He went for his phone.

Theo's gaze followed Ted across the room.

"It's working!" Ted said. "My phone matches the pod's display."

Theo watched Ted as he returned to Jeanette's side.

"Wow." Jeanette said. "Ted, watch Theo's eyes when I move." She walked back and forth in front of the pod and Theo tracked her every movement as if he were watching a tennis match.

"Amazing," Jeanette said. "He's already super smart and super aware!"

"Pink Floyd will do that to you."

"Stop it!"

Ted and Jeanette's phones beeped with an incoming text from Fetal Fantasies. Ted tapped his screen and read aloud to Jeanette.

"Alert! Earlier this evening we experienced a solar flare that triggered massive black outs and communication disruptions, including some major satellites. Please bear with us and do not request support unless it is a dire emergency. Nothing like this has ever happened before, but you can rest assured that every available engineer we have is working around the clock to restore the system to full viability."

Jeanette rested her hand on the pod and sighed. "Thank god Theo wasn't hurt."

Ted glanced at the display screen. "If anything, he's better than ever!"

From that day forward, baby Theo watched their every move whenever they were awake. Often, Jeanette would be involved in another task when the sensation of being watched made the back of her neck tingle. When she turned around to look, Theo's big inquisitive blue eyes would lock on hers.

They kept him in the pod for a few days after his programmed birth date as a precaution, which also allowed them to pick the time and date of Theo's birth and control the astronomical alignment of his birth sign at the moment of his first breath. Jeanette held her burgeoning anticipation to cuddle Theo for a full week so he could be born a solid Scorpio on November twelfth at the exact time of a full moon which also came at sunset on that day. Jeanette thought that the timing of it all as the most magical of synchronicities and a true sign from God.

She made everything ready for the new arrival that day and when the time approached, she and Ted stood before the pod holding hands, watching the display count down to the programmed time of sunset. At six-thirty on November twelfth, the words BIRTH SEQUENCE INITIATED flashed across the pod unit's screen.

A hum and the hiss of pneumatics sent the amniotic fluid draining out of ports at the bottom of the pod while the umbilical tube disconnected and the sensors attached to Theo's head and body retracted into the unit. The top of the pod slid open with a thump, prompting the infant to clear the fluid from his lungs with a cry, announcing Theo's entrance into the world bathed in the pastel pink and orange hues of a brilliant sunset.

Jeanette picked up the squalling baby, wrapped him in a blanket and held him close while Ted put his arm around her and bowed his head. Theo's big blue eyes shone bright and his tiny hands reached for Jeanette's breast.

"I guess it's now or never." She lifted up her blouse and guiding Theo to her nipple.

"He knows what he wants," Ted said. "Can't say that I blame him. Those hormones they gave you made those tatas irresistible if I say so myself."

"Ow!" Jeanette cried out when Theo latched on to her nipple. She held him closer. "Take it easy little one," she whispered.

Theo's demand for breastfeeding filled much of his waking moments. When he became cranky and upset, the only thing that quieted him was his mother's nursing.

When he grew content Theo watched everything they did with full wide-eyed attention.

"He never takes his eyes off of us," Jeanette said one day.

"I feel him watching me, then I turn to see him staring right at me, or I should say right *through* me." Ted said. "Sometimes it feels a little creepy."

"Some of those same thoughts and feelings have crossed my mind, but I dismiss them." Jeanette made a dismissive gesture and went over to the crib. Theo reached for her breasts when she picked him up.

"He's our little prince," she said snuggling him, "and he is always hungry." She held him to her breast. "I can't wait to get him on solid food so we can give my poor overworked boobs a rest."

Ted stroked Theo's soft golden hair which had grown longer along with his feathery eyelashes. "You sure are a beautiful boy. I'm glad you got your mother's looks."

Theo turned from Jeanette's breast to Ted, rewarding him with a huge toothless grin.

"Did you see that? He smiled at me. He knows what I'm saying!"

Jeanette chortled. "He hasn't grown enough for that yet, but I can see how it seems that way with the way he looks at us."

Theo's big blue eyes, golden-blond highlights, and plump baby face combined made him a beautiful angelic looking cherub. Friends and strangers seemed to be unnaturally drawn to Theo's beauty. Everywhere they went, people adored him and spoke in hushed deferential tones in his presence, bowing when his eyes found theirs with his wide-eyed inquisitive gaze.

"It makes me uncomfortable when they bow down to him like that," Jeanette said to Ted under her breath after a group of people had all acted that way when they saw him.

"Who knows?" Ted answered. "Maybe we did make a little baby Jesus. You have to admit, all the adoration does make him happy. I know every parent feels like their kid is special, but Theo *is* special. If you have any doubt, just look at the way people act toward him. They can sense it. Have you ever seen anyone act that way toward a baby before?"

"I can't say that I have, but I've also noticed that he gets upset when he is not the center of attention."

"Every baby is like that. They need the attention and are helpless and totally dependent on us."

"I realize that, but I am his mother and I think he is a little too needy and demanding. It doesn't feel right to me."

As the months passed the two sides of Theo's behavior became more pronounced. When everything went his way, he was the happiest, bubbly, smiling, cooing bundle of joy imaginable, but when he wasn't the center of attention or he didn't get his way, he threw fits until he got what he wanted. Ted jokingly referred to him as Jekyll and Hyde. Both Ted and Jeanette always rushed to give him whatever he wanted to keep the tantrums at bay.

For the longest time, Theo's only means of communicating were his smiles and his tantrums. There didn't seem to be anything in between. The longer this went on, the more concerned Jeanette became about the development of his speech, which she felt should have grown faster.

"He's six months old," she said after calming one of his fits. "He should be babbling and vocalizing more."

"I read that **fifteen percent of babies between the ages of eighteen and twenty four months old are late talkers,**" Ted said. "**They say it can be because they are shy or introverted.** Most babies say their first word sometime between twelve and eighteen months. Einstein didn't speak full sentences until he was five years old. I have no doubt that Theo's late talking is a sign of his budding genius. Give it a little time."

Nothing had changed by Theo's first birthday, so Jeanette raised the issue when she and Ted took him to the Fetal Fantasies clinic for his first year checkup.

"He's a very late talker," Jeanette said, "and I'm getting worried. According to what I read, his cooing is normal, but by this time he should be doing more babbling and making longer strings of sounds like ma ma, ba ba, da da. With Theo it's all smiles and tantrums and the tantrums seem to be getting worse."

Doctor Kennedy, a tall, dark-haired lanky man with expressive brown eyes stroked Theo's golden hair. "It's a little unusual," he said, "but still no cause for alarm. **There's nothing physically wrong with him. In fact he is the perfect baby.**" The doctor made a slight bow. "I'm sure you're giving this sweet little boy plenty of attention, but you can step up your game a little bit. The best way to encourage Theo to talk is to spend time talking and interacting with him. Give him lots of face time and one-on-one interaction. Children learn language by watching and imitating facial expressions. When he coos, say, Oh, are you happy? Are you sleepy? When he smiles, smile back. You can also narrate what you and baby do as you do it. For example, say, Daddy's changing baby's diaper. Baby is holding a spoon. This will help him learn vocabulary. Other things you can do is read a book and point to the pictures on each page, talk about the colors and objects, and sing songs and nursery rhymes. To capture Theo's attention, dance or gently rock him as you sing and act out Itsy Bitsy Spider and Jack and Jill. He will associate movement with words."

"Thanks for the advice," Ted said. "We'll give it a shot."

"I'm already doing a lot of what you're recommending," Jeanette said, "but I'll be paying a lot more attention and putting more effort into it now. Thank you!"

"You have a beautiful boy there." Doctor Kennedy bowed again. "With all the care you have given him, I'm sure he's developing as beautifully inside as he has on the outside." He stroked Theo's hair again, eliciting coos and a smile.

Jeanette and Ted came back six months later with Theo. "We're really getting worried, doc," Ted said, "He's eighteen months old and still no change."

"We did everything you suggested," Jeanette added, "but it's still either coos or cries. I'm at my wits end with his tantrums. He should be vocalizing more by now. I'm terrified that something's wrong. Can you imagine what it would be like if he acted this way when he's bigger?"

Doctor Kennedy held up his hands in a calming gesture. "We'll run some comprehensive tests and take a real close look to make sure everything is still developing normally."

After a day full of tests, scans, and procedures, doctor Kennedy sat with Ted, Jeanette, and Theo in an examination room looking at a screen that resembled the one on the baby pod.

Doctor Kennedy stood, bowed toward Theo and nodded. "I don't know what to tell you," he said as if addressing Theo. "Sight, sound response, reaction time, visual acuity, dexterity. All on target." He continued nodding. "Bloodwork, pulse, respiration, and other vital signs. All optimal. I don't think I've ever seen a more perfect baby. I'll admit that he is running a little behind in his speech development, but physiologically there is absolutely nothing wrong with him." Doctor Kennedy bowed a little lower and stroked Theo's hair while Theo smiled and cooed back at him. "For now, all we can do is give him more time. You never know. He might even surprise us when he does speak."

Six months later, nothing had changed, and if anything, Theo's tantrums had gotten worse. Ted and Jeanette felt panicked and Doctor Kennedy had grown more concerned. They had another check up scheduled for Theo's second birthday when he threw his worst tantrum ever. Nothing that they did could console him and the more they tried the worse he got, finally reducing Jeanette to tears. She dropped to her knees, sobbing with her face in her hands while Theo screamed, then she clasped her hands together and started whispering prayers. Ted dropped down beside her.

"Please god," she said, "help our little Theo. I put my faith in technology and maybe I was a fool for doing that, but my bigger faith has always been with you. We've done everything we possibly can for him and given him everything he ever wanted. I don't know what else to do." She clenched her hands tighter while tears streamed down her cheeks. "I'll do anything you ask and promise to serve you with all my heart and soul."

"Me too," Ted muttered. "Anything to make the crying stop."

The room went silent. Ted and Jeanette looked up wide-eyed to see Theo standing up. His big blue eyes looked brighter than ever before, as if electrified.

He cleared his throat and his little boy voice spoke with surreal authority. "I am your creation that you brought into this world. You have been playing God to me by providing for my every need and desire. Your nurturing of me has proven worthy and I am now the center of your universe. You have earned the privilege to bow down, worship, and serve me with everything you have and all that you are for the rest of your lives."

Ted and Jeanette gasped and glanced at each other for a moment, then turned to Theo and bowed down to him.

YOU ARE WHAT YOU EAT

Bruno Kowalski felt elated lighting his cigar while watching the sign maker he had hired turn on the sign over his newly opened specialty shop called **MAKIN' BACON.** Two happily smiling pigs wearing chef hats bordered each end of it. He crossed his arms over his massive stomach and smiled watching the neon animated pigs tipping their hats on and off from one end of the sign to the other as if saluting each other while the letters of MAKIN' BACON flashed red.

Balding, with a full graying beard, at six foot three Bruno tipped the scale at three hundred pounds and often joked that he earned and deserved every inch and every pound. He loved life and embraced it with gusto, especially his Bacon-Infused Bourbon, Cuban cigars, food, and of course bacon was at the top of his list.

He thanked the sign maker, shook his hand, and gave him a cigar. Tomorrow was International Bacon Day, the perfect day for his grand opening celebration. After the sign maker drove off, Bruno went inside and looked over the shop to insure that everything was perfect, then he went to his back office and looked over the half page ad he had placed in the local paper, as well as on Facebook, Twitter, Linked In, Pinterest, Tik-Tok, and all the other social media sites he could find.

MAKIN' BACON GRAND OPENING

Come join the Labor Day weekend celebration of International Bacon Day at the Grand Opening of Makin' Bacon, Santa Barbara's premier custom bacon shop to revel in your love for bacon. This holiday only comes once a year like Christmas, Super Bowl Sunday, or Thanksgiving, only this holiday is ALL ABOUT THE BACON!

Frying up store-bought bacon and eating it with your eggs isn't gonna cut it. Not this time. Not on Bacon's Day!

Think of all the turkey you eat on Thanksgiving – and you don't even really like turkey, but you love bacon, and you need to do right by bacon on bacon's special day. Don't hold back on bacon's holiday! Break out of your usual bacon routine and give everything you can to bacon on this day of all days, and make bacon proud.

We'll be frying up and giving away free samples of our specialty bacon and have a number of mouth watering demonstrations throughout the day to show our love.

If you're wondering how you can do right by bacon, we'll tell you how and share glorious ways to indulge your bacon love and spread the bacon joy this International Bacon Day! Come join us and discover how to:

- Cure your own bacon
- Eat bacon with every meal
- Join our Bacon of the Month Club
- Make Bacon-Infused Bourbon
- Make Bacon Desserts
- Throw Bacon Tasting Parties
- Create Your Own Bacon Recipes
- Attend Bacon Festivals Or Throw Your Own Bacon Bash

Breakfast, lunch, dinner and snacks. Start off the morning by cooking up a pound or 2 or 3 or 7 of bacon and add it to your meals throughout the day. Bacon and eggs for breakfast. A BBLT for lunch. Candied bacon for a snack and some bacon-wrapped filet for dinner.

It's not hard to make your own bacon. Really, it's not. Imagine being able to determine exactly how your bacon tastes, and exactly how thick each slice is. It all starts with a fresh uncured slab of bacon you can get here!

Bruno looked up from the paper to his computer screen and back, poured himself a celebratory shot of bacon-infused bourbon, then downed it and leaned back in his chair.

Finally, his dream had come true.

They lined up half way down the block before he opened the next day and he had to shoulder his way past a small crowd by the door, apologizing as he went.

"Thank you for coming," he said over and over again. "We'll open in just a few minutes!"

He squeezed in the front door and went to the rear delivery entrance where he found the three young curvy co-eds he had hired to help customers and give demonstrations. Once inside they set up their tables, hung a banner above the door that said GRAND OPENING, and took their places. When all was in readiness, a blonde-haired blue-eyed co-ed accompanied him and handed out samples after he opened the front door with a grand flourish saying, "Welcome to Makin' Bacon!"

Customers milled about the packed store while the checkout line moved non-stop, delighting him to no end.

What a great start!

As the day wore on and the morning's enthusiastic crowd started to dwindle another group of people appeared, seemingly all at the same time, dampening his enthusiasm and harassing his customers as they left with their purchases.

A number of them marched around in a circle carrying signs with slogans like, MEAT IS MURDER, TAKE DEATH OFF THE DINNER TABLE, YOUR FOOD HAD A FACE, and NO ANIMAL WANTS TO DIE, while chanting, "Animals are my friends! I don't eat my friends!"

Bruno hoped they would tire out and go away, but to his horror the antagonistic group swelled in size and grew more vocal with their chants while his paying customers dwindled to a trickle until his checkout line disappeared leaving only the protestors in their wake.

Bruno smiled through it all in spite of his rage. Late in the afternoon when it became clear that his customers had effectively been blockaded by the protestors, he paid his shaken co-eds and ushered them out through the back delivery door to save them from more harassment from the unruly crowd.

Acting as if his adversaries were not even there, Bruno cleared out a space by the front display window and dragged out a butcher's table with a large cherry colored cutting board on top of it. The crowd grew quiet and the marchers stopped and watched him with rapt fascination.

Looking up from his work, he gave them a broad smile and held up a finger before disappearing to the back of the shop, reappearing a few moments later wearing a white apron wielding a butcher knife with the bloodied carcass of a pig over his shoulder.

He giggled hearing the gasps and cries of the onlookers on the other side of the glass, then, cool and methodical, he decapitated the pig and set its dripping head on the end of the table. He followed up by expertly flaying and slicing up slabs of meat in front of the horrified mob.

Five minutes later half a dozen cop cars rolled in and flashing blue lights filled the street. A number of the protesters ran up to the advancing cops and pointed accusing fingers at Bruno, who continued his work unfazed by the activity outside. Two cops stood blocking his front door while others held back the crowd which had grown even larger with curious onlookers.

A heavy set burly looking middle-aged cop barged in through the front door, yelling, "What the hell do you think you're doing?"

Bruno gave him his best smile and pointed to the GRAND OPENING banner above the door, and in his most hospitable voice said, "Welcome to the grand opening of Makin' Bacon. I was just giving a demonstration of the proper way to butcher a pig." He held up a slab of belly meat. "Would you like a complementary cut?"

The confusion passing over the cop's face spoke volumes, but it took a few seconds before any words came out. "You can't," he stuttered. "I mean…" He looked out at the crowd outside pressing in on the barricades that the other cops had set up. By this time an attractive red-haired reporter followed by a cameramen were pushing their way to the front of the crowd.

Bruno winked at the cop. "You can tell your fellow officers to allow the news crews in to interview me," he smiled beatifically. "How could anyone ask for better exposure for an opening day celebration? Did you know that today is International Bacon Day?" He held the slab of meat out closer to the cop. "What kind of cut do you prefer?"

The cop held up his hands and backed away shaking his head. "Give me a minute, will you?" He took a microphone from his shoulder and stepped over by the door where he had a short spirited discussion, then he opened the door and yelled to the other cops to let the news crew in.

Later that evening Bruno kicked up the footrest and leaned back in his easy chair munching on a thick BBLT sandwich, washing it down with a glass of bacon-infused bourbon waiting for the evening news to come up on his big flat screen. He felt elated when he saw images of the crowd in front of Makin' Bacon fill the screen behind a middle-aged conservative looking man at the news desk. The images showed the crowd, then the storefront, ending with a close up of the flashing MAKIN' BACON sign while the newscaster began the report.

"Local businessman Bruno Kowalski held an unusual grand opening of his specialty shop Makin' Bacon on State Street today to celebrate International Bacon Day in a most unusual way that brought unexpected results that have divided the community. Lead reporter Sara Johnston was on the scene with an exclusive report."

The newsroom cut away to video from the front of the store where a stylishly dressed red-haired woman with a pixie cut and green eyes held a microphone in front of a crowd of agitated people.

Bruno rubbed his hands together and lit a cigar.

Sara turned to a tattoo covered woman wearing a black shawl with long dreadlocks, red eyes, and tear streaked cheeks.

ORIANA TELUSHKIN - PRESIDENT LOCAL PETA CHAPTER filled the blue banner at the bottom of the screen.

Sara held the microphone out to her. "What happened here?"

"That sadistic butcher smiled the whole time," Oriana said between sobs. She took a deep breath and continued with a trembling voice. "He rejoiced in the dismembering of an animal!"

Sara turned to the camera and spoke into the microphone. "Some might ask, pigs are bred for food, so what's wrong with eating them?" She paused for a beat, then continued. "Of course, in many Asian countries, we could pose the same question about dogs." She held the microphone out to Oriana who had regained more of her composure.

"We wouldn't serve our dogs for dinner here in a civilized country. Anyone who has spent time around pigs can attest that they are just as loving, intelligent, and capable of feeling pain and suffering as our canine companions, so why do we call one friend and the other food? The biggest difference between pigs and dogs is the way we treat them! Despite the fact that pigs are highly intelligent, sentient beings who feel pain every bit as much as we do, they are regarded in terms of inputs, outputs, and profits by the factory-farming industry. Like many other factory-farmed animals, pigs are not even perceived as living beings. Rather, these animals, who are horrified at the sight and smells of the slaughterhouse and who will fight to save their lives, are treated as mere production units on an assembly line.

"Basic biology tells us that being bred for a certain purpose does not change an animal's capacity to feel pain, fear, or sorrow. Animals who are bred for human consumption still suffer greatly at the hands of factory farmers and slaughterhouse workers.

"On factory farms, sows are no longer allowed to be the good mothers that nature intended. Instead, they are treated as inanimate meat machines, squeezed into narrow metal stalls barely larger than their own bodies, and kept constantly pregnant or nursing. Immobilized, mother pigs are unable even to nuzzle their piglets. Pigs' tails are chopped off and their teeth are cut with pliers—and males are castrated—all without painkillers. At the end of their miserable lives, they get their first breath of fresh air as they are trucked to the slaughterhouse. Finally, they are hung upside-down and bled to death, often, according to slaughterhouse workers and U.S. Department of Agriculture meat inspectors, while still conscious and screaming."

Sara shook her head and spoke again. "So what you are saying is that pigs are emotionally intelligent."

Oriana wiped tears from her eyes and stood up straighter. "Pigs are considered to be even more intelligent than dogs and are capable of playing video games with more focus and success than chimps! They also have excellent object location memory. If they find food in one spot they'll remember to look there next time. Pigs also outperform three year old human children on cognition tests and are smarter than any domestic animal, and animal experts consider them more trainable than cats or dogs.

"Decades of research and scientific observation has shown that pigs are intelligent, complex creatures that have the capacity to experience some of the same emotions as humans, like happiness, excitement, fear, and anxiety. They're able to remember important pieces of information for long periods of time. In the wild, pigs form small groups that typically include a few sows and their piglets. Mother pigs and their babies stay close until the piglets mature. They even prefer to sleep snout-to-snout or snuggled up together."

"Wow," Sara said. "I never knew that!"

"Bringing home the bacon means certain death for lovable, smart, social pigs. Given the opportunity and training, pigs can play some computer games as well as college students, turn on lights and heat in a barn, and perform many other sophisticated activities. As intelligent, inquisitive, and pleasant-natured animals, pigs can be loyal, playful, affectionate companions and have been known to save people from drowning, yet people don't return the favor and many who couldn't stomach the thought of eating their dogs routinely consume pig flesh.

"People who take the time to learn about pigs realize that they aren't emotionless machines whose lives are inconvenient stages on the way to our dinner tables. They are living, breathing, and feeling beings who want to lead their lives free from suffering, just like our faithful dogs and cats do."

Sara turned to the camera. "After hearing that I just might become a vegetarian myself!"

The screen cut back to the news desk where the lead newscaster said, "We'll be back after a commercial break to hear the other side of the story."

Bruno ran to the kitchen for some candied bacon and poured himself another drink while the commercials ran and sat up straight when the news came back on showing the lead at the news desk.

"We here at News Eight believe in balanced reporting," he said. "At the owner's invitation, Sara went into the store to get his side of the story. "Back to you, Sara!"

"We're here inside Makin' Bacon," Sara's voice said while the camera went up and down aisles of the store stopping from time to time to highlight specialty items, ending on a close up of the grand opening banner above the door which delighted Bruno.

How's that for an advertising budget, he thought.

The next shot moved in for a close up of Sara standing beside a smiling Bruno, who stood proudly in his bloody apron.

What a babe, he thought, puffing on his cigar at home. I sure wouldn't mind making bacon with her!

BRUNO KOWALSKI – LOCAL BUSINESS OWNER OF MAKIN' BACON filled the blue banner at the bottom of the screen.

"We're here with Bruno Kowalski," Sara said, "proud owner of Makin' Bacon, who had quite the eventful grand opening today. I understand that business was brisk for you today, Mr. Kowalski, but things turned out a little different than you had planned."

Bruno leaned in close. "Please, call me Bruno."

Sara stepped back and held the microphone out at arm's length. "I understand you had a few unexpected surprises. What happened?"

"I dreamed my whole life of opening Makin' Bacon as Santa Barbara's premier custom bacon shop specializing in rare and exotic bacon cuisine. I chose International Bacon Day to do this which is my favorite holiday. It only comes once a year like Christmas, Super Bowl Sunday, or Thanksgiving, only this holiday, like my store is all about the bacon, which makes it so special! Think of all the turkey you eat on Thanksgiving." He winked at Sara. "I'll bet don't even like turkey, and I'll bet you love bacon."

Sara suppressed a smile. "I'm not so sure about that, but that's not the point. What happened?"

Bruno crossed his arms over his big stomach and rocked back and forth on his heels. "Bacon lovers like myself lined up outside the door and half way down the block before we even got the doors open and business was going like gangbusters until those protestors showed up and threatened my business. My response of course, like any other business owner, was to defend it."

Sara nodded. "In quite the novel way, I might add."

"I was just giving a demonstration of the proper way to butcher a pig."

"Your audience didn't seem to appreciate your craftsmanship. Your critics say that pigs are intelligent, complex creatures that experience the same emotions as humans, like happiness, excitement, fear, and anxiety. They also say that pigs are pleasant-natured animals that can be loyal, playful, affectionate companions. They see them as living, breathing, feeling beings who want to lead their lives free from suffering."

Bruno snorted. "If they are so intelligent, then why are they so easy to raise and slaughter? Aside from that who says vegetables don't feel things. Just because you can't hear a carrot scream doesn't mean *it* doesn't have feelings. Sure, we've all seen the documentaries on Netflix about industrial farming with animals on conveyor belts sliding into grinders, but I believe that if you source your meat ethically – if you have a deep relationship with your food and know where it's coming from, who raised it, what it's been fed, and how its life has been makes it more than okay. All of the pig farmers I source from know the names of all their pigs. As a matter of fact they treat their pigs like gold!"

"So in your mind that makes the slaughter okay."

Bruno sighed. "While they are force-fed, it's only for two seconds per day over the last ten to twelve days of their lives, which comes to a total of two minutes after six months of free-range living. The rest of the time they are looked after and fed every day by the same person. "They're raised much more ethically than any chicken. In fact it's more ethical than most other meats."

"Thank you for your perspective. Any last words?"

"As far as those vegetarian protestors go, to each his own. This is America. Though I do not agree with them I respect their point of view. They are entitled to their beliefs and they need to show me the same respect for mine. It's that simple. Here at Makin' Bacon we take great pains to source ethically farmed animals and we respect the rights and beliefs of others, but no one has the right to force their beliefs on anyone else. We will not change who we are. In my opinion, this controversy points to a wider issue of differing ideologies, but regardless of our differences, it's high time we find a way to co-exist peacefully".

"Thank you Mister Kowal – er I mean Bruno."

Bruno gave her his best smile and pointed to the GRAND OPENING banner above the door. In his most hospitable voice he said, "Welcome to the grand opening of Makin' Bacon. He held up a slab of belly meat. "Would you like a complementary cut?"

Bruno clicked off the remote when the segment ended and a commercial came on. "I showed those fucking granola eaters," he muttered puffing on his cigar and draining the last of the bourbon from his glass.

Bruno knew his actions might have consequences, but he also believed that there was no such thing as bad press. Any publicity, *especially* free publicity, no matter how bad it might look could only help. Some people looked down on meat eaters, but his opening day celebration was a success in spite of the protestors. Bacon lovers were a dedicated bunch and he was counting on them to rally to his side.

His assessment turned out to be more than correct, but he never could have imagined the level of support he got for taking a stand. Makin' Bacon received phone calls, emails, and donations from people across the city and the news segment of his opening day went viral on the internet. Orders flooded in from the hospitality industry from around the world as well as from people in places he had never heard of. He had to hire a full time person to handle all his online business and extra staff to help run the store.

He could barely handle the volume of business that erupted and grew with each passing day. Bruno was forced to work seven days a week for long hours to keep up with the surge in demand until his energy flagged causing him to lose sleep which not only made him irritable, but it made his thinking fuzzy and prone to making mistakes with inventory, staffing, and his finances.

I need to see a doctor about getting a prescription for some speed to get me through this pinch, he thought when he almost fell asleep driving home one night. Better make that a priority.

After a phone call the following morning his doctor sent him to a lab to get a fasting blood panel done and called him two days later.

"I need to see you right away," the doctor said.

"Is something wrong?"

"I can fit you in tomorrow morning at nine. We can talk about it then."

"I have some inventory coming in tomorrow…"

"Nine o'clock. I had my secretary reschedule another patient to get you in, so you can do the same. I need you to come in then."

"Well, I guess…"

"Nine o'clock. See you then."

The doctor hung up.

Bruno didn't know what to expect when he showed up at the doctor's office. The first thing the nurse did was have him step on a scale, take his temperature, and check his blood pressure. She shook her head as she entered his information into an iPad and led him to an examination room where he sat on a white papered examination table wondering and worrying about what the doctor had to say. After a few uncomfortable minutes a grim-faced doctor with dark hair whose nametag said PATEL came in and took a chair across from Bruno beside a computer monitor. He tapped a few keys on the keyboard and turned the monitor toward Bruno.

"I'm going to get right to the point," he said with a stern Indian accent. "You're lucky to be alive and if you don't start taking better care of yourself you won't be for very long." He pointed to the monitor which showed numbers and graphs highlighted in red. "You weigh three hundred and twenty pounds which is grossly overweight, your blood pressure is one hundred eighty over one ten which is considered a medical emergency that can damage your blood vessels and can easily lead to a stroke. Your LDL cholesterol is one hundred thirty milligrams per deciliter which puts you at risk for an ischemic stroke, and on top of all that your fasting blood glucose is one hundred milligrams per deciliter which makes you diabetic."

"What's the good news?"

The doctor's eyes grew wide. "The good news? We need to admit you to the hospital right away so we can try to get these numbers under control."

Bruno held his hands up. "I can't do that right now, doc! I'm at a critical point in my business and I need to be there."

"If you don't listen to me you won't be around to be anywhere. This is nothing to be taken lightly. Frankly, I'm amazed that you're still standing."

Bruno broke into a cold sweat. "It's that serious?" he said in a small voice.

"You need to be admitted right now. I've already made arrangements with the Santa Barbara Cottage Hospital to admit you today."

"How long will I have to stay?"

"There's no way to know for sure."

"Okay, you win, but not today. I need a few days to make some arrangements to keep my business running. I can't afford to let it close. It would ruin me and I have put so much hard work into it."

"I wouldn't advise it."

"Just a few days. I promise."

"For the record, I am dead set against you doing anything but checking into the hospital. Time is of the essence."

"I know, I know, just a little time."

Doctor Patel shook his head. "This goes against my better judgment. I'm going to write you some prescriptions which you need to start taking immediately so we can start getting a handle on your condition - or I should say conditions. Every day you put this off increases the danger of a major cardiac event. I expect to see you in that hospital ASAP!"

Bruno left the doctor's office shaken and in disbelief. He picked up his prescriptions at the pharmacy and called his six employees for a mandatory emergency all hands staff meeting for six o'clock that night. Once everyone arrived, he closed the store and had them gather in the back room.

He had hired four girls, Susie, a short heavy set blonde with a pageboy haircut, Melanie, a stocky tattooed brunette weightlifter, Marsha, a tall curly-haired redhead, and Heather, another blonde with thick arms, a pear shaped body and a ring through her nose. Two gay men who had been his first hires and hardest workers who were always eager to please and who were also lovers engaged to be married rounded out his staff; Bruce, a massively built weightlifter with a buzz cut, and Michael his identical looking partner who was a little taller and wore wire-rimmed glasses.

"Thank you all for coming on such short notice." Bruno dropped into a chair. "I want you all to know that I appreciate all your hard work which has contributed to the ongoing success of Makin' Bacon, and to be honest with you, I owe much of that success to you." He took a deep breath and let out a sigh. "The reason I called you here for this meeting tonight is that I had an unpleasant doctor's visit this morning."

"Oh no," Michael gasped.

"The upshot of it is that I have to go into the hospital for an extended stay."

"For how long?" Heather said.

"I don't know."

"Shit!," Susie said.

They all looked at one another for a long moment before Marsha spoke up.

"What about our jobs?"

Bruno held up his hands. "That's why I called you here tonight. We have a good thing going here and I have confidence in your hard work and dedication to keep it all running and moving forward in my absence. What that means is longer hours for everyone and a twenty five percent raise to motivate you and show my appreciation for your loyalty. I fully understand if this is not acceptable and you want to leave."

Bruce put his hand on Michael's knee. "I think I speak for both of us when I say that you can count us in."

Michael nodded his agreement.

Bruno looked around at the others who all nodded, then he sighed again. "I can't thank you enough. Bruce and Michael, you have been with me the longest and have the most experience, so if you are amenable to it, I'd like to make you co-managers to run things in my absence."

They both sat up straight in unison. "You can count on us!" Michael said.

"Ditto!" Bruce added.

Bruno clapped his hands together. "Thank you. You'll get more details in the next few days while I sort everything out." He stood. "Meeting adjourned. Michael and Bruce can you stay behind to go over some details with me?"

"You bet," Bruce said.

The rest of them filed out the back door, each stopping to wish Bruno good luck. Once they left he turned to Bruce and Michael.

"I realize what a huge responsibility this is, so I think it is only fair to give you both a forty percent raise."

They both stood, smiled, and gave Bruno a hug.

"We appreciate your vote of confidence and promise that we won't let you down," Michael said.

"We'll keep in close contact by phone and email so I can give you direction when needed."

They worked late into the night and from early morning to late night for the next few days going over all the details of running the store, including payroll, scheduling, inventory, bookkeeping, paying bills, and other critical details.

Bruno felt numb and weak on one side of his face, arm, and leg on the third night followed by an overwhelming sense of dizziness and confusion. He struggled to speak and had trouble seeing until a sharp pain gripped his chest and he toppled forward into the blackness.

Bruno awoke to the beep of a monitor, an oxygen mask covering his face, an IV in his arm, and a clip on his finger. A number of electrical connections were taped to his chest that went to more equipment, and tubes ran down his nose into his throat. He turned his head to the side and saw displays monitoring his vital functions.

He drifted in and out of consciousness in that condition hearing the voices of nurses and doctors from time to time as if in a dream, and when he did dream he dreamed of eating bacon in all its novel forms. He lost track of passing days while the length of his conscious time grew until he opened his eyes one morning to see doctor Patel standing over him snapping his fingers.

"Bruno, can you hear me?"

Bruno managed a slow painful nod.

"No need to speak right now. Just listen so I can update you on your condition. Your heart has suffered irreparable damage and we are waiting and hoping for a donor, but the chances of that are remote. The waiting list is quite extensive. Do you understand the situation?"

Another nod.

"We weren't sure you were going to pull through, but by some miracle you did. Now that we finally have you stabilized we'll be removing your oxygen mask and moving you out of the ICU into your own room." He looked at his watch. "I will be meeting with a team of cardiologists this afternoon to discuss our treatment options."

"Thanks doc," Bruno whispered.

Doctor Patel returned later that afternoon. "Bruno, are you awake?"

Bruno blinked his eyes open. "Yessir."

Two other white jacketed doctors stood with doctor Patel.

"This is doctor Symington," Patel said gesturing toward the older gray haired one, "our leading cardiologist and this is doctor Owen." He nodded toward a lanky, dark, curly haired man. "Our top endocrinologist."

Both men bowed toward Bruno.

"We've been discussing the complexities of your case," doctor Patel said, "and thought we should continue discussing your options in your presence so you are fully aware of any risks and rewards."

"I'm all ears."

"At first we talked about the possibility of a mechanical heart," doctor Patel said, "but doctor Symington advises against that."

"In some cases, an artificial heart transplant can be permanent," Symington added, "and it could last for several years, but the likelihood of surviving more than four years is less than sixty percent. The record for the longest time living with an artificial heart is five years. We also talked about trying to salvage your heart valves, but your heart is far too damaged for a mechanical valve. We also have the added worries of the fact that you weigh over three hundred pounds and your high blood pressure can further damage your cholesterol clogged blood vessels which can trigger an ischemic stroke.

"While mechanical valves can last a lifetime, they come with an increased risk of blood clots necessitating the use of the blood thinner warfarin. On the other hand, biologic valves, which are made from pig or cow tissue, do not increase the risk of either bleeding or clotting but will wear out sooner."

Bruno perked up hearing this. "Pig valves?"

Symington shook his head. "I'm afraid your heart is too damaged for that too. Your best chance would come from a donor heart, but the waiting list is prohibitively long."

Bruno felt a flash of inspiration. "What about a pig's heart? I know for a fact that pig hearts are just like human hearts. I remember hearing on the news about a guy who got a pig heart transplant."

Symington rubbed his chin thoughtfully. "The University of Maryland School of Medicine transplanted a genetically modified pig's heart into a fifty seven year-old man back in January of two thousand twenty two, demonstrating that a genetically-modified animal heart can function like a human heart. After surgery the transplanted heart performed well for several weeks and showed no signs of rejection, but unfortunately the man passed away two months after receiving it.

"Porcine heart transplants are not approved by the FDA, but in this man's case they granted an emergency authorization for the surgery through its compassionate use provision which is sometimes used when an experimental medical product, in this case the genetically-modified pig's heart, was the only option available for that patient who was faced with a life-threatening medical condition." He pursed his lips and looked to doctor Patel, then back to Bruno. "In the condition you are in, you could conceivably qualify for that."

Bruno could barely control his excitement. "Please, tell me more."

"They used a new drug along with conventional anti-rejection drugs designed to suppress the immune system and prevent the body from rejecting the foreign organ. The pig heart was also genetically modified to reduce the chance of rejection, which is an issue with both human heart transplants and previous attempts to use animal heart transplants.

"They modified ten genes in the pig heart. Four were knocked out. Three of them responsible for producing antibodies that cause rejection, and one gene was knocked out to control the growth of the pig and its organs in an effort to make the hearts more acceptable to the human immune system to prevent rejection.

"Traditionally, a donor heart is matched to the recipient by blood type and body size. Heart transplant recipients also have to take immunosuppressive medications to prevent the immune system from rejecting the new heart by suppressing the body's normal immune response to a foreign object, but these drugs can have side effects including infection or an increased risk of some cancers."

Bruno pressed a button and raised the back of his bed up into a sitting position. "Instead of having a heart like and ox," he bragged, "I'd have the heart of a pig. This will work for me. I *know* it!"

"Why do you think that?" doctor Patel said.

"Pigs are my spirit animal!"

Doctor Owen looked skeptical and slowly shook his head. "You can't be serious. Even if this harebrained scheme worked, your diabetes adds more complications, among them peripheral vascular disease, neuropathy, and trauma. Tissue damage, gangrene, or death can occur, and any existing infection could spread to your bone."

"What about antibiotics?"

"If the infection can't be stopped or the damage is irreparable, amputation of your toes, feet, and lower legs might be necessary."

"We can cross that bridge if and when we come to it," Bruno said. "What do you say, docs? At this point we have nothing to lose and we just might make medical history."

Three months later Bruno sat up straight in his hospital bed grinning from ear to ear as the evening news came on the flat screen mounted high up in the corner of his hospital room. The lead newscaster began, "In our top story tonight, the essence of bacon is in the air once again in a mind-bending contradiction of major proportions that local businessman Bruno Kowalski, the proprietor of the controversial, newly opened specialty store, Makin' Bacon calls the blessing of blessings. Once again our own Sara Johnston is on the scene at the Santa Barbara Cottage Hospital with an exclusive report about this landmark achievement in medical history."

The newsroom cut away to Bruno's hospital room where Sara stood beside him holding a microphone, and beside them stood his proud doctors. Sara's sparkling green eyes lit up with excitement which looked even more pronounced in contrast to her red pixie cut and teal dress. Bruno's smiling staff stood on the other side of his bed wearing T-shirts emblazoned with the happily smiling Makin' Bacon pigs wearing chef hats.

"You made medical history," Sara said into the microphone, "and once again you find yourself in the middle of a controversy that your critics are calling an ironic contradiction. Can you explain what all the fuss is about?" She held the microphone out toward Bruno, keeping him at arm's length.

Bruno gave his best smile. "First off, let me clarify one thing." He gestured toward his staff and his doctors. "*We* made medical history. I would not be here talking to you now without the dedication of my amazing staff and the incredible doctors that I have been blessed with. Doctor Patel, you and doctor Symington need to take the spotlight here for our historic accomplishment. Tell them the details of the miracle you have achieved."

Symington nudged Patel forward and Sara held the microphone out to him.

Patel cleared his throat. "The first genetically modified porcine heart was transplanted into a fifty seven year-old man back in January of two thousand twenty two. The transplanted heart performed well for several weeks, but the man passed away two months after receiving it."

"Now about that contradiction that people are making such a stink about." The camera went to a closeup of Bruno who puffed his chest out. "I am the Baron of Bacon and master butcher who knows more about the anatomy of pigs than anyone alive and it is common knowledge that a pig's heart is similar in size and anatomy to a human heart. I admit to the irony, but there is an even greater irony behind that. Aside from the fact that I was practically on my death bed with few options, because of my intimate connection with pigs I was absolutely sure that this transplant would work. The doctors were all skeptical, but I insisted that I knew it would work."

"What made you so sure?" Sara asked.

Bruno's smile filled his face and a wistful look came to his eyes. "Pigs are my spirit animal!"

Bruno awoke in a cold sweat one morning a few days later to the smell of bacon. Disjointed images from the remnants of a fitful dream of a pigsty on a vendor's farm flitted through his mind. He wiped his forearm across his sweaty forehead and stopped mid-wipe.

Was it his imagination or did his sweat actually *smell* like bacon? He licked the crook of his arm and was rewarded with the mouth watering satisfaction of the unmistakable salty taste of crisp, juicy bacon.

Jeez, he thought. I must be having withdrawals.

He pressed the button on the side of his bed raising it to an upright position while puzzling over his experience, torn between an uncomfortable low level fear, fascination, and the urge to keep licking himself.

His taste buds won out and he licked some more. How long had it been?

He heard voices from the hall and pulled the covers up over his shoulders to hide his embarrassment the moment before doctor Patel and doctor Symington came through the door.

"When can I get out of here?" he blurted. "I miss my store. I miss my bacon."

The two doctors looked at each other. "We'd like nothing more than to do that," doctor Patel said, "but there are still anomalies in your bloodwork that doctor Owen is concerned about related to your diabetes and the condition of your extremities. We are doing everything within our power to avoid any negative outcomes and part of that entails keeping you here under close observation."

"But we've broken records and you said my heart is doing great and exceeding your expectations."

"That part is true, but the complications from your diabetes require the utmost care and attention. You are a living breathing example of medical history and it would be a shame to lose you to something that in many respects is unrelated to your heart."

"How long am I going to have to stay here?"

"It's hard to say at this point. We have to be sure that you are absolutely stable before we can release you."

Bruno felt uncomfortable over the next few weeks. His skin itched and became thick and leathery like one giant callus and coarse wire-like hairs sprouted from his ears and chin. His ears also became hard and elongated with points forming at their tops while his nose swelled up and grew misshapen and flattened at the end. It oozed bacon smelling wetness while his finger and toenails grew curved and clawlike.

He cut himself while struggling to trim a thickened fingernail one day and instinctively put his finger in his mouth to stop it from bleeding all over everything. The delectable heightened flavor of the best bacon he had ever tasted filled him with euphoria followed by the now familiar conflicting feelings of fear and fascination.

"What the hell is happening to me?" he said when doctor Patel came to his room followed by doctor Symington and doctor Owen.

"That's the part of your bloodwork we have been studying and trying to figure out," doctor Owen said. "Something appears to have triggered an unusual hormonal reaction in your endocrine system."

"What can you do about it?" Bruno said, feeling his chest tighten. His nose wiggled and cold sweat broke out on his forehead.

Doctor Symington looked down, shaking his head. "We're still puzzling over that, but unfortunately complications from your diabetes have escalated to the point where we are forced to implement more radical invasive lifesaving interventions."

Bruno's chest tightened more to the point of borderline pain.

"In spite of the fact that your new heart has exceeded our wildest expectations, your diabetes has advanced, presenting the dangers that we feared the most." He took a deep breath and looked up. "I'm afraid we're going to have to amputate both your legs."

"My legs?"

"We had to make sure you stabilized before proceeding with that, but the clock is ticking. We have to act fast to avoid further damage from vascular disease, neuropathy, tissue damage, bone infection, and gangrene, all of which can end your life prematurely."

Bruno felt speechless as the information tumbled through his mind, then the words came as if on their own accord. "What will you do with my legs after you cut them off?"

"They will be disposed of in a sterile, biologically safe sanitary manner."

Bruno shook his head no. "I would like them returned to me."

Symington frowned. "That's an unusual request, one that I am quite sure does not fall within hospital policy."

Bruno's mouth watered. "They're *my* legs, aren't they?"

Author's Note

The germ of this idea came into my head awhile back and I decided to begin working on it on September 3, 2022, when I committed to writing the story, and to my amazement during the course of my research I discovered that this was International Bacon Day!

PORTALS

He had no idea when and where it all began and when and where it would end, and he didn't care. Nothing mattered to him except the moment. To be more accurate, it was his fascination with the ever-changing passage through the eternal moment of his tenuous existence, for he was an interdimensional traveler flying through realms that defied description.

On this night he passed through a reality that blazed prismatic with multifaceted vivid colors, movement, and details, each holding him spellbound like brilliant animated gems, each reflecting their unique color, hue, personality, and emotion. The impact of his exquisite living visual tapestry and the depth of its detail altered his senses in ways he could not comprehend, but that didn't matter either. He felt awe and gratitude for the constant stream of blessings they brought him.

His world shifted and came into focus with astounding clarity. Sunshine turned into darkness and cool night air flooded his senses as he moved through the night, stopping every few minutes to listen and sniff when a light breeze kicked up, carrying with it exotic smells and sounds. Unintelligible voices came to him through the darkness.

They often spoke to him, but he had no grasp of what they said because he couldn't understand their language. *His* language was something entirely different, consisting more of feelings, conceptions, and emotions as opposed to the babble and limitations of words. In this ecstatic flow of perceptions where time and space became fluid, he sailed through extraordinary vistas of sight, sound, and sensation replete with powerful emotional content.

He remained stone-still and spellbound in his bliss, overwhelmed at the center of his awareness while the world around him fluttered, pulsed, buzzed, chirped, chittered, rustled, whispered, and vibrated, coming to him in crystal clear, yet inexplicable ways. He did not hear this symphony from his surroundings in any recognizable way. What he "heard" he felt as one and the same vibration at the center of his being. The sound came to him weak, but what it lacked in auditory energy felt enhanced and amplified by the fluttering sensation inside of him.

Though a mystery in and of themselves, their uniqueness paled in comparison to the rich visual tableau he immersed himself in with full attention, exploring the differing pathways that brought these all-encompassing, multi-layered sensations.

A fluttering breeze brought him an unexpected avenue of information in the form of two antennae extending from his head bringing their own unique vibrations to his feeling-hearing sense, and on that same quivering breeze came the scents of life that drove his insatiable hunger.

His added sensations and heightened awareness led to the realization that along with his antennae he had six legs and a triangular head with bulging eyes. Three smaller eyes in the middle of his head sensed light while two bigger compound eyes detected movement and depth and his neck felt oddly fluid.

At the moment of his epiphany reality strobed and he moved outside of time and space where expanded, but still limited perception no longer applied. Colors with hues that defied description bombarded him with multicolored geometric progressions that could be microcosmic quantum expressions or unfolding galaxies. Within these realms he inhabited tiny beings devoured by bigger beings devoured by still bigger beings with long ethereal stomachs that passed him into bizarre realms that both amazed and terrified.

Different abstract sounds filled the night air with calls, cries, twitters, pulsating whoops, rasps, and buzzes, and for him there was no difference between the infinity expressing itself outside of him and the infinity that he travelled through inside of him.

It was all one and the same and at times he felt fully present and aware in two places at the same time, often in different times and dimensions.

After traversing the realities of predator and prey he flew first as larger entities, then as smaller, fast moving beings that darted, flew forward, backward, up and down, all the while feeling the hum of his entire being centered in his fluttering heart, propelling him into sublime and exquisite high frequency realities exploding with neon luminescent pastel manifestations.

His body quivered and his insides teetered on the verge of full release of everything it held while he soared between agony and ecstasy. Each embrace awed him with a palette of feelings and emotions that ranged from heavenly bliss to hellish maddening terror. He grew vaguely aware of others around him crying out from time to time in fear or bliss as they passed through their own realities and he felt his essence connected to theirs.

A mild breeze slipped over him and the pungent smells of his companions filled his senses. Though in darkness, his eyesight had an acuity beyond its power in daylight and his ears moved as if raising from his head. He focused on the sounds of his companions along with a number of smaller beings moving in the underbrush, up in the trees, and buzzing in the air around him, each with their own distinctive volume and pitch.

He strobed again and the force pulled him into another dimension, causing his awareness to shift and adjust to a new point of reference. Low to the ground. His vision refocused, sharper than it had been moments before.

He closed his eyes, shook his head, and opened his eyes to see fur covering him. Hands gone. Now paws. A tail. He willed it to move and it flexed as naturally as moving a finger, then his tongue found a mouthful of big sharp teeth and his sleek body felt like he belonged in it.

Leaping to his feet, he reveled in his strength and agility when he lunged forward, first slinking, then easing into a loping gait. Muscles flexed beneath skin and fur as his heightened balance carried him with light-footed ease.

He experienced a keen sense of smell and a feeling of brutal power in his four limbs, along with a strange dichotomy of being part of this form, yet removed, floating along with it, both participant and observer. Swift and silent, he moved stopping only to listen and sniff the night air, sorting through its myriad scents. Desire gnawed in his gut, driving him onward in search of anything to satiate the burgeoning hunger that threatened to overwhelm him.

Rapid-fire flashes drew him into damp darkness where he hung upside down, sensing others hanging close. He blinked, trying to get his eyes to adjust, but they didn't function well. His frustration elicited a high-pitched squeal that bounced off the bottom and sides of his enclosure, giving him a clearer image of his surroundings that more than made up for his diminished sight.

He let go with his claws and dropped, spreading delicate wings, flitting through the darkness, navigating narrow passages by letting out short cries that echoed back to him, guiding him out into a clear night sky. Thin, kitelike wings allowed him to hover, stop and turn with astonishing precision.

Uttering a short burst of sound, his sensitive ears "saw" a soft, fluffy being fluttering ahead. He zeroed in on it and made a quick cut, catching and swallowing it before flying off in search of more. When he became thirsty he dipped low over the surface of a small pond and skimmed along the top scooping water into his mouth.

He hunted more smaller soft flying beings and ate his way through the night, enjoying himself between meals by exploring the high-speed acrobatics his agility provided him. When his light-sensitive eyes caught the first indications of the approaching day, he flew back to the dark safety he had emerged from to find a comfortable spot to hang upside down again among his brethren and strobed into a darkness that swallowed him as if he had dropped into the mouth of a much larger being.

No feeling.

No sound.

No sight.

No awareness of his surroundings.

He felt only the sensation of falling further into blackness until he became aware of sparkling gold lights that captivated his attention far off in the distance. He willed himself toward them, and as he drew closer he sensed the beat of the lights matching the rhythm of his heart.

The pulse grew and turned into the beat of flapping wings until he flew through the growing light, huge wings beating the air, then spreading and sailing on the wind, while his vision swirled in geometric patterns bringing a flurry of images that filled his awareness until he drew up out of the shadows through a long dark tunnel, closer to the source of lights.

His vision took on razor-sharp definition while he hovered, enjoying the ease with which he stayed aloft, then he tucked his wings in close and plummeted, thrilling at the speed he dropped at. The earth rushed toward him until a crash seemed imminent, then he spread his wings and swooped inches from the ground relishing the intensity in each detail of the terrain. His momentum carried him back up until the wind caught him again, and with a few powerful beats of his wings he shot upward, once more, riding the breeze, diving again and again, each thrill as satisfying as the last. The wind, his heightened vision, sense of control and timing all felt natural until he hovered at the edge of it all, his sight and hearing vigilant.

His entire being soared and a feeling of oneness filled his heart while he sailed on the winds and the world spread out beneath him like a carpet. Elated, he ascended higher and the breeze carried him until he once again became formless, riding the wind before his vision grew hazy and his world grayed.

His pulse boomed in his ears, matching the thump of his heart and the wind gusted, first blowing past, then pulling him closer toward the lights until their intensity increased and the strobe overtook him, once again altering his perceptions.

Swirls of murky light played across his mind like colored searchlights through fog and he felt relaxed and at peace, yet highly aware. Disembodied voices that didn't come from any particular direction blended with the rest of his surroundings and flowed toward flickering golden lights that appeared to pop on one by one, coming toward him along a row. Spiraling mists swayed in a gentle rhythm, then parted, leaving him slipping somewhere between what felt like sleep and dreaming.

Soon after drifting into this netherworld, the forces carried him along until he floated downward and his awareness shifted until he opened his eyes in darkness, once again recognizing his heightened smell and sharpened vision. He explored his surroundings with his enhanced sight, smell, and focus, detecting things he had never sensed before, adding to his insatiable curiosity.

The wind gusted and his head shot up catching an acrid scent and a flood of adrenaline made him jump as though touched by a live wire, then his vision blurred, and his head fell back, giving him a brief view of blue sky before darkness closed in again.

Countless smells mingled like colors in a painting. He separated each one in his mind, discarding those he knew to be familiar, focusing on two that felt out of place. The unmistakable stronger scent of his brethren and the unfamiliar scent of intruders, cut across everything else like a bold stroke of red in an otherwise gentle pastel.

He tracked both scents to the spot where they met. Here the sour, acidic odors of his companions felt overpowering and the darker smell pressed in stronger. He moved his head, swaying from side to side to sniff the air and opened his eyes to the sights, sounds, and odors of his brethren while the malevolent scents of the foreigners grew stronger.

He stifled the urge to panic and paralysis rendered him helpless. His mind remained alert, but his body stayed rigid, refusing to obey his impulses. He breathed in deep willing himself to stay calm and accepting.

Dizziness passed through him, followed by a clearing of his faculties, numbness, and a sense of tranquility and detachment, as if his thoughts drifted toward an entirely different dimension when the smiling faces of his liberators loomed over him.

His mind shifted as if floating further above his body.

His heart beat faster.

He felt several foreign presences, each so distinct he felt he could reach out and embrace each one, so he opened his heart and gave himself up; a smaller celestial body coming under the influence of a larger one and saw the brilliant gold flashes of his fellow travelers leaving this dimension punctuated with their screams of ecstasy.

In the next moment the burning wet of his pungent baptism splashed over him and in a blinding flash the world around him melted, its substance dribbling to the ground like streams of different colored waxy fluids that took on the form of snakes slithering toward him.

Nausea came and passed until he saw the familiar swirling geometric patterns in a smoky blue haze that grew in intensity until a door of blinding light opened and a breeze came carrying him across the sky.

Sparks flew through the air and his body rose, as though lifted by a wind that grew stronger and he rose faster, disappearing into the blackness while stars raced toward him in dizzying swirls as he spun still faster, hurtling through the air like a demented comet. He instinctively spread his wings, laughing in delight as he couldn't remember ever feeling freedom such as this.

He hurtled toward the closest star while spiraling lights filled his vision and the sensation of flying apart overwhelmed him. As he blazed out of this world he put his palms together and the fullness of his non-verbal emotional comprehension coalesced into the blossoming expansiveness of his spirit embracing all that is with the essence of his realization.

I am star dust, manifest in the wind, the rain, the rivers, the lakes, and the oceans. I am the rocks and the mountains and the ground that gives life. I am the grasses in the fields, the flowers, trees, vines, bushes, funguses, mosses, and molds. I am all of the creatures of the earth who crawl, slither, walk, fly, and swim, for I am a keeper of the cosmic fire that burns within every one of them. I am in all of the plants and all of the animals because I come from the infinite heavens that I now return to because I am a child of the stars.

Though incomprehensible to him, the last sounds he heard were these.

"God damn, Mickey, look at that motherfucker twitch!", then a slapping sound, followed by, "We did the world a favor by getting rid of another lowlife fucking worthless piece of shit stinking up the streets and polluting everything!"

The very last thing he heard was the staccato sound of their laughter which also consumed him until he made identical sound feelings laughing uncontrollably along with them as he passed through the consuming flames of white-hot transformation in awe and ecstatic joy, sailing through this portal, embracing whatever the great mystery held for him in the next realm of his existence.

TIME AFTER TIME

Rick slid his hands down the curves of her firm body, reveling at their touch while she loomed over him, dark hair cascading above him, her green eyes blazing with passion while she helped him out of his pants. The musky scent of cloves and cinnamon filled his senses when her breath came hot and wet in his ear, then her lips met his. Her hungry tongue thrust itself into his mouth as she raised her hips and slid on top of him and ran her nails down his back while he thrust upward to meet her.

He felt pure ecstasy a moment before something sharp cut his tongue, causing him to jerk his head back. The soft skin pressed to his body grew bristly, her fiery green eyes receded, and her beautiful aquiline nose transformed into the black-nosed snout of a wolf full of sharp canine teeth. Her ears grew out and the bristly feeling against his skin became fur. Claws slit open his back while her emerald eyes remained locked on his, hypnotizing him like a cobra with its prey. Rows of jagged teeth sank into the soft flesh of his throat while his arms and legs flailed and his life ebbed into oblivion. In his dying agony he remembered the pocket watch clutched in his hand. He held it up and pressed the button on top.

Rick sat straight up in bed, slick with sweat, heart racing, his whole body trembling. "Holy shit! What the fuck was that all about?" He took deep breaths to calm himself then showered to clear his head, followed by a solid shot of espresso to set him right. *Time for the Ren Faire*, he thought. *Been waiting for this all year!*

He put on his costume and studied himself in the full length mirror in his bedroom. He stood tall in his ruffled white shirt, tuxedo trench coat, and matching vest. A wide black leather belt with a huge silver buckle held it all together above pantaloons and knee high boots. He adjusted the black ostrich plume on his leather musketeer hat and stepped back. *Almost there,* he thought *Today he would find a gold pocket watch with a gold chain…*

The thought sent images from his waking nightmare flitting through his head and he smiled. *That's where that watch in my weird ass dream came from! I went to sleep thinking about it because I knew I was going to be looking for it today at the Ren Faire.*

Another picture perfect San Diego day made the Balboa Park Ren Faire feel all the more magical when Rick passed armored knights checking wristbands at the entrance. A group of hard-bodied little pixies with fairy wings bounded by followed by a tall beautiful woman he thought of as their fairy godmother. She looked royal with waist length curly golden hair topped with a glittering tiara. Large sparkling gossamer wings complemented by a jewel encrusted wand, rings, and bracelets accented an elegant, frilly, puffy sleeved lavender dress making her look like a bigger than life beautiful exotic orchid.

I know what I would wish from her and her little pixies. Rick smiled and waded into the crowd moving through a group of bodice clad busty bar wenches. More armored knights passed carrying jousting lances and shields, while minstrels sang and played guitars, mandolins, and flutes.

He wanted to see it all, but the jingling of a brightly colored jester wearing a cap and bells hat juggling at the entrance to the Village Marketplace drew him in. He had all day to see everything, but he wanted to find the right pocket watch to put the finishing touch on his costume first.

Rows of artisans, merchants, and vendors displayed medieval fantasy themed wares while glassblowers, leatherworkers, blacksmiths, candle makers, and pottery throwers demonstrated their skills. Children giggled having their faces painted and their hair braided.

Violin music called his attention to a brightly painted, elaborately carved, four-wheeled horse-drawn gypsy wagon with an awning fashioned from tapestries hung with gold tassels at the end of the longest row. A battered looking wooden sign dangled over the entrance to the stall with the words "Time After Time" carved into it in Old English lettering. Ancient looking hourglasses hung from the awning and shelves full of intricately carved clocks, wrist, and pocket watches, and sun dials of all shapes and sizes, as well as other exotic timepieces filled rows of expensive looking glass curio cabinets.

The biggest, most elaborate curio case caught his attention and his heart swelled when he spotted the gold pocket watch.

That's it!

His mind erupted with his morning dream within his moment of revelation that the watch he was looking at was the one he had seen in his dream, then the sweet smelling scent of cloves and cinnamon came to him followed by a deep throaty, Slavic sounding accent. "It looks like you have found what you were looking for."

He pointed to the watch. "That's mine!"

She giggled. "I know."

"How do…" He looked up into her emerald eyes, meeting her tranquil gaze and she rewarded him with a broad beautiful smile from full lips, then he took in her curves, dark cascading hair, and the intoxicating essence of cloves and cinnamon.

"I am a gypsy. I know these things."

He pointed at the watch again. "Can I see it?"

"Of course." She reached down into her cleavage and pulled out an old fashioned key from her bodice. She opened the cabinet, took out the watch and pressed it into Rick's hand, holding his hand with her two slender hands a moment before letting go. The watch felt warm and tingly in his hands and glinted gold when he held it up to study the finely detailed runes inscribed on it. He looked back up at her, then at the watch again, back and forth, torn between his fascination with the watch and her enchanting presence. Rick found himself fantasizing about taking her in his arms, burying his face between her breasts and…"

"That would be very nice," she said in a low sultry voice.

"What did you mean when you said you knew the watch was mine and how you're a gypsy that knows these things?"

"It is part of my family, part of my culture, part of my genetics. I cannot explain it, but this magic has always been part of my life." Her lips parted in a suggestive smile and she looked him up and down, then she fluttered her long eyelashes. "I can read your mind and I know exactly what you want."

Rick felt his face flush hot. "I'm not sure I believe in any magic, but now I'm starting to wonder after the dream I woke up to this morning."

"I know."

Pleasant tingles rippled over his scalp, arms, and legs, ending in his groin. He ran his finger over the inscriptions on the watch. "What do they mean?"

She took the watch from him and held it in her palm, running her finger over the runes. "It is an incantation to activate the powers of time to let you fulfill your desires." She winked at him. "It can turn time back in case you need to correct your mistakes." She held up the watch with her thumb poised over the knob on top. "All by pushing a button." She dangled the watch by its chain and lowered it into Rick's hand.

His attraction to her grew stronger at the touch of its warmth. *This is too weird*, he thought. *No way she can read my mind or sell me this time travel bullshit.*

"You don't believe me." Her eyes brightened and she pulled the watch back. "I can show you."

She looked around, then took him by the hand. Her touch fueled his excitement and he submitted, thinking, *this can't be happening. Shit like this doesn't happen in the real world.*

She led him up carpeted steps into the back of her wagon behind her stall and sat him down on the edge of a warm, plush pillow covered bed. Trinkets, charms, jewels and an assortment of other objects hung from a ceiling painted in an elaborate nature scene. Everything inside the womb-like interior was painted in vivid detail with every color imaginable.

She held the watch between her praying hands and muttered a low incantation while slowly rotating her hips. Rick felt an overpowering sense of déjà vu when she stepped in closer and pressed the watch into his hand.

She writhed in slow sensual movements as she slid on top of him, pressing him down into the softness beneath him. Rick slid his hands down the curves of her firm body, reveling at their touch while she loomed over him, dark hair cascading above him, her green eyes blazing with passion while she helped him out of his pants. The musky scent of cloves and cinnamon filled his senses when her breath came hot and wet in his ear, then her lips met his. Her hungry tongue thrust itself into his mouth as she raised her hips and slid on top of him, and ran her nails down his back while he thrust upward to meet her.

He felt pure ecstasy a moment before something sharp cut his tongue, causing him to jerk his head back. The soft skin pressed to his body grew bristly, her fiery green eyes receded, and her beautiful aquiline nose transformed into the black-nosed snout of a wolf full of sharp canine teeth. Her ears grew out and the bristly feeling against his skin became fur. Claws slit open his back while her emerald eyes remained locked on his, hypnotizing him like a cobra with its prey.

Rows of jagged teeth sank into the soft flesh of his throat while his arms and legs flailed and his life ebbed into oblivion. In his dying agony he remembered the pocket watch clutched in his hand. He held it up and pressed the button on top.

Rick sat straight up in bed, slick with sweat, heart racing, his whole body trembling. "Holy shit! What the fuck was that all about?" He took deep breaths to calm himself then showered to clear his head, followed by a solid shot of espresso to set him right. *Time for the Ren Faire*, he thought. *Been waiting for this all year!*

THE DIARY OF CARMILLA McTAVISH

Twelve year old Kayla's long dark hair ruffled in the breeze coming from inside the ancient castle in Ireland, and her button nose twitched at the musty scent of long ages past. She felt like a dream had come true and couldn't contain her excitement standing there in the massive oak doorway gazing up with her big brown eyes at the vaulted ceilings looming within.

She had heard whispers of castles being haunted by ancient kings, princesses, knights, and other members of the royal court, and imagined its hallowed halls buzzing with magic, dragons, castle intrigues, and sacred quests like the ones she had been reading about and imagining herself in from as far back as she could remember.

Ralph her father nudged her gently inside from behind. "What do you think?"

She looked back at him and smiled. His brown eyes twinkled behind his glasses. His close-cut beard and smile went up into raised bushy eyebrows under a mop of salt and pepper hair.

"It's magic daddy."

"We're glad you think so." Her mother Donna stepped past them into the foyer on long, slender legs. She stood a little taller than her husband and attracted attention with her raven-haired locks, and expressive dark brown eyes whenever she came into a room. She held out her hands and spun like a ballerina, then leaned down toward Kayla. "This place is living history," she half-whispered.

As if on cue, a frail white-haired old crone dressed in black wearing a frilly white apron seemed to float out from the shadows. "Welcome to castle McTavish," she said in a reedy voice. "We've been expecting your arrival."

Donna shot a glance to Kayla and her father and smiled. "You must be Lady Farnsworth."

"At your service." She bowed and smiled through yellowed teeth. "And this must be Kayla." Lady Farnsworth put a trembling hand on Kayla's cheek and gave it a gentle squeeze. "What a pretty little lass you are." Her eyes sparkled. "It will be nice to have a sweet little thing like you around."

Her hand dropped to her side and she looked to each of them one at a time. "Don't hesitate to call on me. I'm here for anything you might require. All you need do is ring a bell and I or one of my staff will be there to tend to your needs."

"Thank you," Ralph said bowing in return.

"Come along." Lady Farnsworth took Kayla by the hand. "Let me give you a tour of Castle McTavish before lunch is served."

Donna and Ralph looked at each other and smiled, following them down long chandelier lit hallways with arched ceilings. Elaborately patterned Persian carpets led them past stone walls covered with ornate tapestries, large paintings, and alcoves holding suits of armor, marble statues, and busts. Lady Farnsworth narrated as they circled the castle, stopping from time to time at doorways to large rooms off the main hall and cross hallways, describing their history and function.

She stopped in front of the largest portrait at the center of the hall portraying a portly bearded man dressed in extravagant Elizabethan finery emblazoned with embroidered golden crests. "Castle McTavish's owners include warlike bishops, politicians, social reformers, agricultural innovators, philanthropic wives, pre-Raphaelite painters, furniture collectors, writers, and war heroes, all of them connected with royalty, ambassadors, and prime ministers." She held her hand out toward the picture. "The first McTavish named Angus came here from Scotland. He was a chamberlain and protector of Mary Queen of Scots. After his passing he was often seen by servants walking around the castle. Since that time there have been accounts of hauntings and rumors of strange happenings like bells ringing, other mysterious figures wandering the corridors, a baby's cry in the night, and stories about a young girl about your age appearing to visitors rumored to be Carmilla, the granddaughter of Angus McTavish who disappeared under mysterious circumstances. She is rumored to have drowned, but they never found her body.

Kayla looked up at the old woman wide-eyed. "Have you ever seen or heard any of these things?"

"Oh, yes," Lady Farnsworth said, "but lest you be frightened by these tall tales, I have been passing them on for many years the way they were passed down to me from generation to generation. I have no doubt that anything I ever experienced has been nothing more than dreams stimulated by an overactive imagination."

"Kayla has quite the imagination herself," Donna said. "She has spent many hours role playing in Dungeons and Dragons games."

"And a bit too much time playing the same kind of video games on the internet," Ralph said.

"Castle McTavish should help remedy that," Lady Farnsworth said, starting forward again. "Dinners are served by candlelight in the original dining room, just as it was in the old days, with pre-dinner drinks served in the Drawing Room or Fountain Garden, and to keep with tradition there are no TVs, radios, internet, or cell phone service. Just wonderful food, relaxed and friendly service, and lazy breakfasts served until eleven as well as picnics by the lake."

Kayla stopped and let go of the older woman's hand "What?"

"We want to cultivate your imagination on its own," her mother said, "without all the distractions of games and technology that separate you from the real world. Your imagination is free to run wild here by itself, away from all that toxic garbage that pollutes everything online."

Kayla clenched her fists at her sides and scowled.

"Here you can spend some time living like they did in the old days," her father said, "and experience history the way they did back then. You are a good reader and there are plenty of books and history for you to explore here."

"It will do you a world of good," her mother added.

The three stood in awkward silence for a moment until the old woman took Kayla's hand and led her forward again. "I think you might have a little change of heart when you see your room."

"I doubt it."

Lady Farnsworth led them up a winding staircase inside of one of the castle's biggest towers which had four bedrooms. "You get the nursery Kayla."

Before Kayla could respond the old crone pushed open a heavy creaking door to a large room in the top floor of the castle with a steep oak roof. A four poster canopied bed sat against a wall on the left across from ancient oak dressers and a large brass candelabra sat on a heavy wooden table beside it. Shelves lined with ancient volumes filled a third wall. The furthest wall had a picture window overlooking a large lake surrounded by a vast green meadow against a backdrop of gently rolling hills.

"Look at all those books," Donna said. "I'll bet you'll learn a lot more about history reading them than you would from any web sites."

Kayla stood immobile for a moment, transfixed. Her parents exchanged worried glances until she breathlessly said, "I feel like I belong here."

"That's wonderful, sweetie," Ralph said.

She moved slowly into the room, touching the bed and running her hand along the dressers and books along the shelves, stopping to examine some of the titles before drifting to the window where she gazed out at the fairy tale scene spread out below her. "I feel like I've been here before," she said half to herself.

After a long day touring the castle grounds, the lake, and the meadows surrounding it, Kayla and her parents ate a candlelit dinner in a large stately dining room furnished with old carved oak, large curved cabinets, and chairs cushioned with crimson velvet. Four windows looked out over the lake and the walls were covered with tapestries. Looking royally down from great gold frames, life-sized figures wearing ancient costumes engaged in activities like hunting, hawking, and other festivities. The décor and atmosphere felt magical to Kayla in spite of her underlying resentment at the lack of online access and the missing comfort of her cell phone.

Her mood lifted later that night after she kissed her parents good night and went to her room, finding it bathed in a warm glow from the candelabra reflecting off the picture window, highlighting the bookshelves. She spent some time examining and cataloging the books in her head, forming a mental list of which ones she wanted to read, and what order she wanted to read them in. When her mind started to drift, she climbed under the coverlet in the big canopied bed where she wrestled with her fading resentment of missing her computer games and the growing comfort and novelty of her castle room at the top of the tower.

She drifted off into an uneasy sleep thinking about Rapunzel until sometime later when she saw her room and the furniture the way it was when she drifted off, except that it looked a little darker. The shadows of the bedpost danced upon the wall and she saw something moving around the foot of the bed.

It grew brighter and she saw a young girl standing there wearing a loose dress holding a book. Red hair covered her shoulders and looked haloed with golden highlights in the soft light. She stood stock still without the slightest stir of respiration until their eyes met, then she drifted into the middle of the room where her entire face glowed with the same radiance as her hair, as if lit by a book she held to her breast.

She turned toward the bookshelf and the light from her face illuminated the center, growing brighter as she floated toward it. She looked back once as if reassuring that Kayla saw what she was doing, then she slipped the glowing book into the middle of the other volumes lining the shelf and disappeared into the wall.

Kayla awoke with a start smelling candle smoke and looked over at the candelabra to see that the candles had burned out, leaving only trailing smoke. Disbelieving what her eyes and nose told her, she reached out and felt the remaining warmth of soft wax.

She awoke to daylight feeling lightheaded. The memory of the book and her ethereal vision intruded into her thoughts. She wished she could actually read it, then she dismissed the idea as its appearance had only been a vision in a dream.

"I saw Carmilla," she blurted when she met her parents for breakfast out on a landscaped veranda overlooking the lake.

Her mother set down her cup of tea. "Who?"

"She visited me last night in a dream. You know, the ghost of the granddaughter of Angus McTavish. She appeared near the foot of my bed and showed me a book."

"That's wonderful," her father said.

Her mother smiled. "I see your imagination hasn't wasted any time fitting in here."

"I can't wait to tell Lady Farnsworth to see what she thinks."

"Thinks about what?" the old woman said bringing a breakfast tray to the table for Kayla.

"Carmilla!"

"What about her?"

"She visited me last in my dream and showed me a book."

Lady Farnsworth blinked as if she'd been slapped, then quickly regained her composure and set the tray down in front of Kayla. "She showed you a book?"

"We told you Kayla has quite the imagination," her mother said.

"I should say so," the old woman said, hurrying off.

Kayla went to her candlelit room that night thinking about her dream of Carmilla. In her excitement she struggled to fall asleep and thought herself still awake when she became aware of the solemn pretty face of a girl her age with green eyes, red hair, and a thin face with an aquiline nose that she knew to be Carmilla. She studied Kayla from the side of the bed, kneeling with her hands under the coverlet. Kayla gazed back at her with a sense of ecstatic wonder, then Carmilla caressed Kayla with her hands and laid down beside her on the bed drawing her closer, smiling. Kayla felt a deep happiness until Carmilla's eyes fixed on hers. The intensity of her gaze shocked Kayla and she sat bolt upright letting out a short scream.

Carmilla slipped down to the floor and slid under the bed whispering, "Read my diary," in a Scottish brogue. The room grew darker until Kayla couldn't see anything but Camilla's green eyes hovering near the foot of the bed, then the door opened and she left the room.

"How did you sleep last night?" her mother asked when she joined her parents for breakfast.

"I don't feel like I slept, but I know I did."

Her father looked down from over the paper he had been reading. "More dreams?"

Lady Farnsworth came to the table with Kayla's breakfast.

"Carmilla came again," Kayla said. "It felt like she was right there in bed with me."

Lady Farnsworth set Kayla's breakfast on the table with trembling hands. "Did she say anything?"

"She told me to read her diary."

Lady Farnsworth stood up straight and her eyes grew wide. "What diary?"

"That's the funny part. I've looked at all the books in the room and there is no diary, so the only thing I can think of is the book she showed me in the dream."

After Kayla and Lady Farnsworth left the room, Donna leaned in closer to Ralph and said sotto voce, "That's the same kind of dream two nights in a row. Should we be concerned?"

"You know what an active imagination she has," Ralph said going back to reading his paper.

"Maybe it's just me," Donna said, "but have you noticed that Lady Farnsworth seems to be a little rattled by Kayla's dreams too?"

"Give it some time. Kayla's still excited about being here, and if you look on the bright side, she hasn't complained about missing her online games."

Kayla went to her room that night and found the candelabra once again waiting for her in the glowing room. The golden reflection of candlelight off the window made a book in the center of the bookshelf where Kayla had seen Carmilla put one shine with a brightness that suffused it with a light of its own. She felt it silently calling to her, so she went to the shelf and saw a book that hadn't been there before.

Shaking with trepidation she pulled it from the shelf. It felt unnaturally warm and heavy in her hands. It had a beautiful, thick, leather bound cover decorated with gold book corners engraved with intricate scrollwork and a gold inlay title written in elegant calligraphy that said:

THE DIARY OF CARMILLA McTAVISH

She held it close to her bosom feeling its warmth and shuffled over to her bed as if in a trance, anxious to see what secrets it held.

The candles flickered out and a silvery light from a full moon filled the room, coalescing into a wraithlike figure that grew more solid with each passing moment.

When Carmilla came to the bedside Kayla saw that she had a slender figure and wore a soft silk dressing gown embroidered with flowers and lined with thick quilted silk. She moved gracefully as she climbed into bed beside Kayla, gently took the diary from her and pressed her hand on Kayla's. Her green eyes glowed as she looked into Kayla's.

Her complexion looked rich and brilliant. Her features were small and beautifully formed, her eyes large, green, and lustrous, and her hair, magnificently thick and long hung down about her shoulders. Kayla put her hands under it feeling wonder at its weight. It was exquisitely fine, soft, and a very rich red with something of gold. Carmilla sat up straight with the diary in her lap and spoke in a sweet little voice.

"I must tell you my vision about you," she said in a Scottish brogue. "It is so very strange that you and I should have this time together in so vivid a dream, that each of us see, I you, and you me, looking as we do now, when we are both from different times. I come to you from a confused and troubled dream, and find myself in my room, yet though mine, it is unlike my nursery."

"But how did you get here?" Kayla whispered. "What time did you come from?"

Carmilla sighed. "I can't explain it, except to say that I have been waiting for you. I saw you most assuredly in my dreams as I see you

133

now; a beautiful young lady with long dark hair, the cutest button nose, and those wondrous big brown eyes. When I climbed on the bed and put my arms about you, you sat up screaming. I was frightened and slipped down to the ground and lost consciousness." She looked down at the diary in her lap. "I'm so sorry. I didn't mean to scare you."

Kayla felt herself trembling while struggling against a strange attraction that terrified her to her core, but her fascination with what was happening overrode her fear. "It – it's okay. Are you going to read to me?"

"I can tell by the way you are shaking that you've had more than enough for one night," Carmilla said softly. "My story is frightful and it does not have a happy ending, but I am dying to share it with someone who would understand it. Being the person who comes to me in my dreams, I think you are the only one who can." She reached out and held Kayla close for a moment and whispered in her ear, "Good night, darling, it is very hard to part with you, but good night. Tomorrow I shall see you again." She sank back on the pillow with a sigh, and her fine eyes followed Kayla with a fond, melancholy gaze before she disappeared with the words, "Good night, dear friend."

Kayla went down to breakfast feeling puzzled by the night's events which seemed hyper-real while happening in her room in the night, but now here on the veranda in the light of day part of her began to doubt that anything had happened at all. She wanted to hear Carmilla's frightful story with the unhappy ending, even though the thought of hearing it filled her with foreboding.

"Did you have any dreams last night?" her mother asked.

Kayla looked down, unsure of what to say, then she looked up at the expectant looks on her parent's faces. "Nothing that I can remember."

Donna seemed relieved, but concern showed on her face. "Are you all right, honey?"

Kayla nodded and forced a smile. "I'm fine, mom. I think I'm still getting used to living without my online friends."

Her mother looked over at her father as if asking permission. "I think it might be a good idea to get you out of here for awhile. How about we go into the village and do a little shopping to change things up for you a little. What do you say?"

Ralph nodded his approval.

"Sure! Sounds like fun."

Kayla couldn't contain her excitement when they passed a dress shop displaying traditional Scottish dresses in the window with tartan plaid patterns in checkered designs of woolen threads in different colors that formed vertical and horizontal designs. As a reward for foregoing her gaming activities, Donna bought her ankle length skirts made from tartan fabric with matching sashes and shawls, **frilly white blouses with puffy sleeves, and several pairs of** shoes called ghillies.

Kayla went to her room that night and climbed into bed to the glow of the candelabra and soon drifted off to sleep. At some point during the night the reflecting candlelight from the window highlighted the diary in the center of the bookshelf, once again suffusing it with a light of its own. She felt its calling and was about to retrieve it when Carmilla appeared and turned toward the shelf where the light now coming from her face illuminated the diary. It grew brighter as she floated toward it and in the next moment she climbed into bed beside Kayla holding it close. Her glowing green eyes looked into Kayla's as she took her hand and pressed it against the diary.

Something inside of Kayla shifted when she felt the warmth from the book send her into a strange division that often happened in her dreams that she thought of as astral projection. In one moment she was outside of her body watching herself, and in the next she was in bed beside herself as if she had become Carmilla. She looked to the side and saw that she had red hair, then reached up feeling a thin face and aquiline nose that didn't belong to her.

Though she no longer saw Carmilla, she felt her presence and was aware of the warmth of the diary laying in her lap. The sweet little voice of Carmilla spoke with its familiar brogue from somewhere inside of her.

"Let's read it together."

Kayla opened the diary and began to read the text written in flourishing calligraphy while the voice of Carmilla narrated the words, reading along with Kayla.

"My story and the cursed story of Castle McTavish started with the evil deeds of my Grandfather Angus and became darker still by the acts of his daughter, Lady Mircalla." Carmilla paused before whispering, "My mother," which sent a chill from Kayla's ear sprinting down to the base of her spine.

Her hands shook as she continued reading.

"As the story goes, the McTavishes hired 40 men from the O'Reilly Clan to train their men in the new methods of warfare. After the training sessions the O'Reilly men were invited to a feast, however the men were unaware that the dark and evil McTavishes poisoned the food so they could avoid paying the bill.

My mother, guided by my grandfather practiced the dark arts of the occult and together the bodies of the O'Reilly Clan were hidden within the walls of the castle in a chamber known as the Bloody Chapel.

Following that, a murder between a Priest and his brother took place instigated by my mother and her strange practices during a high mass when the priest planned to expose their deeds.

This added sin upon a sin against the clergy required the sacrifice of a virgin to consecrate the dark offering."

"Me," Carmilla's voice reverberated through Kayla. "But in my purity I could not remain trapped in those lower worlds. It was foretold that I would return when the time was right, something I have been trying to do for many centuries – until now."

Kayla felt herself pushed further down into a dense, muted place.

"My mother gave me a potion that deadened me. I couldn't speak or move, but I could see and hear everything while she performed a ritual sacrifice at the lake with me as the offering during a full moon to appease the malevolent spirits she invoked. The official version of the story says that I drowned in the lake, but my body has never been found."

Kayla wanted to wake up and run from the bed, but sleep paralysis kept her immobile.

"If you doubt my words," Carmilla continued, "ask Lady Farnsworth. In 1922 workmen found an oubliette in a secret dungeon hidden behind a wall in a corner of the Bloody Chapel. When they explored it further they made a horrific discovery. There were enough human skeletons amassed on top of wooden spikes that it took three cartloads to remove them for a proper Christian burial."

Kayla placed her astral arms around the neck of her inert physical body and drew her close, laying her cheek against its cold cheek, murmuring near to its ear with words that were not hers. "Think me not cruel because I obey the irresistible law of my fate. My wild heart bleeds with yours amidst the rapture of my great humiliation. I live in your warm life, and you shall sweetly die into mine. I cannot help it. As I draw near to you, you also draw nearer to me."

Carmilla's words sounded like a lullaby and soothed any resistance into a trance until she withdrew her arms, leaving Kayla to wake alone in the darkness, screaming silently.

"Well, look at you," Ralph said, when Kayla appeared for breakfast later that morning dressed in an ankle length tartan skirt and sash over a frilly white blouse with puffy sleeves.

"My goodness, you are certainly playing the part," Donna added.

"Who's playing?" Kayla said, speaking with a brogue in a sweet little voice.

Lady Farnsworth stood stock still and white-faced, clutching the tray with Kayla's breakfast.

"You've certainly done an amazing job role playing this character," Ralph said, "and you have that accent down, as if you've been speaking it all of your life."

"I have."

Donna set her tea down and looked sideways at Ralph. Lady Farnsworth remained motionless.

"That's very good," Donna said. "Very convincing. Now come sit down and have some breakfast with us, Kayla."

"I'm not Kayla."

"Okay," Donna said. "I'll play along. If you're not Kayla, then who are you?"

"Carmilla."

Lady Farnsworth dropped the tray in a loud crash of broken plates and clattering silverware. Ralph and Donna jumped. Kayla showed no reaction.

Ralph stood, moving to help Lady Farnsworth. "You can stop the silliness now, Kayla," he said with an edge in his voice. "You've upset Lady Farnsworth."

Another server arrived to help Lady Farnsworth and Ralph sat back down again.

"I'm not being silly," the sweet Scottish voice said. "Kayla's gone. I'm Carmilla."

Her mother slammed her fist on the table, rattling everything. "Kayla stop it. "You're scaring me!"

Ralph put his hand over Donna's. "Calm down, honey." He looked to Kayla. "Sit down and have something to eat with us."

"I'm not hungry right now and I don't want to upset anyone, so if it pleases you, I'd like to go back to my room and do some reading."

"I think that's a good idea," Ralph said. "Go on up and lie down and relax. We'll send something up to you for lunch so you won't get hungry."

"I think all the excitement and the big changes in her environment have been a bit much for her, and she hasn't had any friends to play with, so she's retreated into her imagination," Ralph said after Kayla left. "We'll keep a close eye on her, but let's give her some time to herself. I'm sure she'll adjust after she settles in a little more."

"I'm worried," Donna said. "I've seen her acting out and dressing as lots of different characters, but none like this. It frightens me."

Ralph nodded. "If we don't see any change in the next day or so, we'll call a doctor."

"Maybe we should call one now."

"Let's give it a little time."

Kayla stayed in her room all day reading old books, barely reacting when her mother brought her lunch late that afternoon. When she didn't come down for dinner, Donna checked in on her and found her sound asleep, still dressed in her tartan outfit with a book in her lap, so she let her daughter sleep, peeking in on her a few times during the night until her own exhaustion sent her into her own deep slumber.

As soon as she awoke the following morning, Donna went to check on Kayla and found the room empty, so she went downstairs hoping to find Kayla having breakfast with her father on the veranda. Neither of them were there and the dining area felt unusually quiet. Lady Farnsworth was nowhere to be seen.

Donna went back to the kitchen and caught the attention of one of the helpers, asking, "Where is Lady Farnsworth?"

"I haven't seen her this morning…"

"Have you seen my husband and daughter?"

"The helper looked at her, but didn't answer.

"Is something wrong?"

After an uncomfortable pause, the helper said, "I'm not sure what to say, but there has been a tragedy down by the lake."

"A tragedy? What do you mean?"

"A drowning. They found the body of a young girl."

"My God!" Donna cried and rushed out of the kitchen, heading down to the lake toward a small crowd amidst the flashing blue lights of police cars. She pushed through to the front of the crowd, finding her way to Ralph who stood staring at the body of a young girl being covered in a sheet. Her heart caught in her throat when she saw the ankle length tartan skirt, matching sash, and frilly white blouse Kayla had been wearing.

"Kayla!" she screamed in a choked cry.

She stumbled forward and pulled back the sheet, fainting at the sight of the pretty face of a young girl who was Kayla's age with long red hair, a thin face, an aquiline nose, and vacant green eyes that stared off into emptiness.

LOVE POTION NUMBER NINE

Maury Perkovich, President and Chief Scientist of Peptide Passions stood among a group of scientists and investors outside of his Torrey Pines lab in San Diego. Tall and gangly, his receding hairline and stooped shoulders from a lifetime of peering into microscopes made him look older than his forty two years, but his precise scientific mind made up for his lackluster physical appearance.

He pushed his coke bottle bottom glasses higher up on his hooked nose, shuffled through some papers and looked up, smiling through crooked teeth. "It looks like you have all signed your non-disclosure agreements, so we can begin the demonstration." He handed the papers to Rebecca, his petite red-haired secretary assistant who wore a white lab coat and sported a bob cut.

His audience consisted of a number of buttoned down executives and scientists, and a few attractive elegantly dressed women who reeked of money and privilege. It took all of his willpower to keep from ogling them, their beauty, and their near perfect figures, and none held him more spellbound than Margaux Lavigne, a French perfume heiress who was also a supermodel who graced the covers of every fashion magazine he could think of. With full lips, high cheekbones, and striking feline eyes that held you in their spell, Margaux would not only be the perfect person to partner with, she was the epitome of the perfect spokesperson for his discovery he called Love Potion Number Nine after the old song that had been playing non-stop in his head since making his discovery.

"Love stimulates all of your happy chemicals at once," he said punching the access code to his lab on a panel by the door. "That's why it feels so good, but our brains evolved to motivate reproduction, not to make you feel good all the time. That's why the good feelings don't last."

He ushered the group into his lab which bustled with white coated undergraduates leaning over microscopes, beakers, test tubes, Bunsen burners, centrifuges with blinking lights, computers, and an array of other electronic equipment. He led the group to a large rack of marked glass terrariums holding scampering rats. The lowest rack held smaller terrariums that had single rats in them. The ones on the right were labeled BOYS and the ones on the left were labeled GIRLS.

"When you understand your happy chemicals, you can build realistic expectations about love. That's the best way to make it last." He looked back and winked at Margaux who scowled at him, then he turned back to his rats to hide his discomfort.

"Each happy chemical rewards love in a different way," he continued. "When you know how each one is linked to reproductive success, the frustrations of life make sense."

"Are those rats who are by themselves unhappy rats?" a white-haired man in a dark suit asked.

"That's very perceptive of you." Maury squatted down to the lower shelf in front of the side marked GIRLS. "We used CRISPR technology to edit the genes and made some targeted genetic mutations on these knockout rats to make the males more passive and the females more aggressive."

"Frankenrats!" the man said.

A few giggles passed through the group with the exception of Margaux who rolled her eyes.

"Please forgive this next little brutality." Maury removed the cover from one of the smaller terrariums marked GIRLS, "but it will only last a few moments before I intervene." When he reached in the female rat backed into a corner and stood up on its haunches, hissing. He pulled his hand back and dropped a small piece of cheese into the container. When the rat lunged for it, he put his hand in behind it and snatched it up by the tail. It twisted, turned, and screeched while trying to bite him.

Margaux's eyes grew wide, then she wrinkled her nose and pressed her hands to her ears.

Maury held the rat at arm's length while Rebecca removed the cover from a single male's terrarium. The male rat huddled into a corner while Maury reached into the pocket of his lab coat and pulled out a small atomizer.

He lowered the squirming female into the opposing corner and released it. The moment he let go, it leaped across the terrarium and attacked the cowering male which let out high-pitched screeches.

Margaux's hands flew to her ears and she yelled, "Stop it!" in her own shrill scream.

Maury reached in and pulled the attacking female away from the bloodied male, once more holding the squirming rodent at arm's length. "Observe," he said in a monotone. He held the rat higher and sprayed the atomizer into its face.

It went limp and scattered gasps passed through the group, then he lowered it into the terrarium again across from the male.

This time the female remained immobile for a few seconds before creeping toward the male which let out pitiful whining sounds as it approached. When the female crawled on top of the male it gave out a short screech until the female started licking the wounds it had inflicted, then the two became calm as the female snuggled up to the male and groomed it, giving extra attention to the wounds. The group observing the phenomenon oohed and aahed, eliciting a broad smile from Maury until he stole a glance at Margaux who looked expressionless.

"I know much of this is proprietary," a short man in a tan suit with salt and pepper hair said, "but what can you tell us about how it works?"

Maury went to the lab door and held it open while his secretary beckoned to the group. "If you'll all kindly follow Rebecca and join us in my conference room, I have a presentation prepared for you to answer questions you might have along with some refreshments."

"I don't think I have an appetite for anything after that grotesque display," Margaux grumbled as she walked past him trailing the scent of an exotic perfume.

Maury smiled and stifled a retort.

Rebecca led the group to a conference room at the end of the hall where they filed in with Maury following behind. Most of them went to a table at the back of the room filled with coffee, pastries, fruit, sandwiches, and a vegetable platter.

A huge flat screen with a stylized image of cupid drawing his bow against a blue background took up most of the wall at the other end of the room. The words LOVE POTION # 9 blazed above it in red centered between two hearts with arrows through them.

Margaux went straight to a chair at the back of the room at the end of a long conference table. Maury poured himself a cup of coffee and stood at the other end of the room beside the screen while the rest of the group took their seats.

He cleared his throat once everyone settled in and picked up a remote control. "Love triggers a cocktail of neurochemicals because it is highly relevant to survival, but it can't guarantee nonstop happiness. It feels like it can while you're enjoying the cocktail, so your brain learns to expect that." He pressed a button on the remote and a graphic of scientists and lab equipment filled the screen.

"Scientists in fields ranging from anthropology to neuroscience have been asking about this for decades and it turns out the science behind love is both simpler and more complex than we might think. Needless to say, the scientific basis of love is often sensationalized, and as with most science, we don't know enough to draw firm conclusions about every piece of the puzzle. What we do know is that much of love *can* be explained by chemistry, so if there's really a formula for love, what is it and what does it mean?" He pressed the remote and an animated cartoon of a man ogling a beautiful woman came onscreen showing him with a beating heart and smaller hearts floating up out of him.

Maury winked at Margaux and she rolled her eyes in response.

"Think of the last time you ran into someone you find attractive," he continued. "You may have stammered, your palms may have sweated; you may have said something asinine and tripped spectacularly while trying to saunter away. Chances are, your heart was thudding in your chest. It's no surprise that for centuries people have thought that love arose from the heart, but as it turns out, love is all about the brain, which in turn makes the rest of your body go haywire."

The cartoon man's heart rose up from his chest into his head.

"According to scientists, romantic love can be broken down into three categories: lust, attraction, and attachment. Each category is characterized by its own set of hormones stemming from the brain. Though there are overlaps and subtleties to each, each one is characterized by its own set of hormones. Testosterone and estrogen drive lust; dopamine, norepinephrine, and serotonin create attraction; and oxytocin and vasopressin mediate attachment."

The cartoon man onscreen floated over to the woman and the two embraced in a flurry of hearts.

He pressed the remote and a graphic of a human body filled the screen with a red heart covering the genital area. "The testes and ovaries secrete the sex hormones testosterone and estrogen, driving sexual desire."

He pressed the remote and the heart in the graphic floated up from the genital to the head. "Dopamine, oxytocin, and vasopressin are all made in the hypothalamus, a region of the brain that controls many vital functions as well as emotion."

Another click brought up a graphic of a brain with hearts designating the prefrontal cortex, the hypothalamus, and the pituitary areas. The magnified chemical structures of the hormones related to each area completed the diagram. "Several regions of the brain affect love. Lust and attraction shut off the prefrontal cortex of the brain, which includes rational behavior which can be problematic. Love can often be accompanied by jealousy, erratic behavior, and irrationality, along with a host of other less-than-positive emotions and moods."

He pressed the remote and the cartoon man and woman appeared onscreen again. On the right side of the screen the man's eyeballs were popping out of his head and a stream of hearts rose up from his genital area resembling an erection. The sexy blushing woman on the left side of the screen had glazed eyes and a stream of hearts going down into her genital area.

"The first phase of falling in love is the lust or desire phase which is the craving for sexual satisfaction. During this phase, men and women both release healthy amounts of testosterone and estrogen. Regardless of gender when these hormones are present at healthy levels, the reproductive system is regulated, energy levels increase, and sex drive is heightened." Maury held up a finger. "Pheromones are odorless chemicals produced by humans and detected by the nose of other humans that play a role in the lust phase and help to initiate the initial desire. During this phase, the primary objective is to have sex rather than form an emotional connection."

The pattern of the hearts onscreen moved up into the heads and hearts of the characters. "Adrenaline, dopamine and serotonin are involved in the attraction phase. Adrenaline is released during the human stress response and plays a role in enhancing attraction and arousal of humans causing the heart to beat faster and stronger, resulting in a surge of energy that focuses attention solely onto the potential mate. It can also heighten feelings of anxiety or nervousness and butterflies in the stomach.

"Dopamine plays a role in motivation, addiction, attention and desire. Once released, it produces a feeling of happiness and bliss. Dopamine is also released in response to cocaine and sugar which are both highly addictive. During the lust phase, dopamine levels increase which can lead to an addiction to the person that is desired. High levels of dopamine are also associated with norepinephrine which is another chemical messenger that increases excitement and focus on another individual.

"Serotonin plays a role in maintaining mood balance, appetite, sleep, memory, sexual desire, and sexual function. During the attraction phase, serotonin levels decrease which can result in sleeplessness. Low levels of serotonin have been linked to individuals with Obsessive-Compulsive Disorder and may also be the reason why individuals in the attraction phase of love obsessively thinks about their potential partner. Even though it decreases during the attraction phase, sex can cause serotonin levels to increase again."

The cartoon man and woman onscreen floated toward each other and the flurry of hearts increased.

"During this attraction phase one can experience feelings of euphoria and exhilaration in their craving for union with the other human they desire. Since hormones associated with the stress response are released during the attraction phase, individuals can also experience physiological changes like sleeplessness, increased energy, loss of appetite, rapid heart rate, and accelerated breathing. Often considered the honeymoon phase between two partners, this phase usually only lasts a few months or less before the attraction fades or the attachment phase takes over."

The onscreen characters slammed together in an explosion of hearts resulting in a passionate embrace of kisses.

Maury smiled and wiggled his eyebrows. "Once the attraction phase settles down dopamine, serotonin, and adrenaline levels return to normal and another phase begins. The two major hormones involved in the attachment phase are oxytocin and vasopressin which play a role in social and reproductive behaviors in humans.

"Oxytocin, referred to as the love hormone is released during the attachment phase in correlation with physical touch and results in an increase in the happy hormone dopamine. This is why the area of the brain associated with the feeling of reward and pleasure is activated when oxytocin is released during contact with another human. Hugging, kissing, cuddling, and sex, can boost oxytocin levels which enhances the bond between both partners. Vasopressin is another hormone released after physical touch that initiates the desire to stay with that particular individual and develops a strong emotional attachment that brings a feeling of calmness, security, a desire to protect one another, emotional union, and comfort."

"Hormones usually work internally and only have a direct effect on the individual that is secreting them. Pheromones, unlike most other hormones, are ectohormones which are secreted outside the body and influence the behavior of another individual by inducing activity in other individuals like sexual arousal."

He stopped for a beat to let his words sink in and pressed the remote, displaying three different chemical structures with their names beside them on the screen. "In our studies we discovered that a substance called AND, which is a progesterone derivative caused swelling in the erectile tissue of female noses indicating that it might be a functioning pheromone. That along with another pheromone known as androstadienone which appears to be a component of male sweat that increases attraction, affects mood and cortisol levels and activates brain areas linked to social cognition. Finally, androstenone, secreted only by males, has also been tested for its potential role as a pheromone. According to some studies, it increases a woman's libido."

Maury pressed the remote and the image of cupid drawing his bow with LOVE POTION # 9 above it between the two hearts with arrows through them filled the screen behind him.

"We used CRISPR-based peptide technology to facilitate a customized, high-throughput *in vitro* hybrid peptide that combines AND, androstadienone, and androstenone which capitalizes on the best properties these three pheromones have to offer." He clapped his hands together. "And that, my friends is the basis for the formulation of Love Potion Number Nine."

A smattering of applause came from the group and when it settled down, Maury asked, "Any questions?"

"How do you know that it will work?" Margaux asked.

"I think my demonstration with the rats has proven quite conclusively the power of this unique hybrid pheromone peptide."

"That's great for lab rats, but you don't know anything about its effect on humans, do you?"

"It's only a matter of time. All of our projections indicate…"

"And you genetically altered the rats which in my book invalidates the results of your twisted little demonstration."

"True," Maury said. "That admittedly biases our results, but on the contrary, instead of invalidating our results, it in fact amplified them."

She turned her nose up. "At the expense of those poor disgusting rats, I might add."

"We're running out of time here, but I can gather the data from our studies and projections and share them with you." He made a show of looking at his watch. "Are there any other questions?"

The white haired man in the dark suit held up his hands and stood.

"Not at the moment." He nodded. "Thank you for a most interesting demonstration." He turned and headed for the door.

"Most interesting." Another rose from his chair and followed the first man out.

More than half the group followed suit, including most of the women. Margaux remained in her chair.

"I'd like copies of those studies and projections too," one of the two remaining women said. She looked to her companion and nodded, then they rose together and left.

Maury clasped his hands together. "Anyone else?"

The rest of the group who had stayed behind raised their hands.

Maury rocked back and forth. "Good! Good! I'll see that they go out to everyone this afternoon. More questions?"

When no one responded, Maury said, "Well then thank you for coming. We'll be sure to keep you apprised of new developments as they arise."

The last of the group clapped half-heartedly and headed for the door with the exception of Margaux who stayed rooted in her chair, apparently lost in thought. Maury had feelings of anticipation mixed with dread that made him feel queasy. If he could win her over he wouldn't need any other investors. The fortune that her father's company held and her alluring supermodel persona presented an ideal partnership. She would indeed be the perfect spokesperson for Love Potion Number Nine.

He cleared his throat and bowed low to her in deference when she approached, enthralled with her beauty. "I am deeply sorry that Romeo and Juliet offended you."

Her face scrunched up. "Romeo and Juliet?"

"That's what I named them. In spite of the brutality of the demonstration I really do care for them very much."

Her expression turned into a scowl and when she spoke, her voice shook with anger. "I would not have come if mon pére had not insisted. If you want to know the truth I think your Romeo and Juliet are nothing more than disgusting rodents, and as revolting as I think they are, your cruel abusive treatment of them is even worse!"

She clenched her fists and leaned in close. "I have all I can do to keep myself from slapping your face."

"But – but – I can show you!"

In spite of her anger, her passion, closeness, and the smell of her excited Maury. Sweat trickled down his armpits, his heart thumped in his chest, and he felt himself getting hard while imagining his own hormones going haywire inside of him.

How he wanted her.

"There, there," he whispered. He put one hand in his pocket and rested the other on her shoulder caressing it in an effort to calm her, but it had the opposite effect.

"Get away from me you little toad!" She shrieked, then backed away raising a fist and turning her nose up to him like a petulant child refusing to eat something she hated.

Acting more from instinct than anything else Maury caught the wrist of her approaching fist and his other hand came up out of his pocket clutching the atomizer of Love Potion Number Nine. Before he could even process the thought he sprayed her in the face scoring a direct hit to her upturned nose.

She shrieked and he let go of her wrist, watching her in stunned amazement. Her hands dropped to her sides and a series of puzzled rapidly shifting emotions played across her face, then her shrieks softened to dog-like whines which faded into long passionate moans that ended in a warm open smile and like flipping some hidden switch, a completely opposite reaction flowed over her, moving from revulsion to adoration.

"Mon chéri," she whispered throatily.

Maury's world froze in an infinite moment of stillness while his heart raced. Fear swept through him.

"Mon chéri," she moaned again, holding her arms out wide.

Her words jolted him and the last of her rigid body language melted into open submission. He remembered the atomizer in his hand and dropped it back into his pocket. She moved toward him and he held out his arms feeling shocked, confused, and vulnerable all at once.

She pressed her perfect body to his and squeezed him in a firm embrace, then she pressed her groin to his in a grinding motion bringing instant arousal while her tongue hungrily entwined his in a hot, passionate dance of soft flesh.

Instinct took over and he arched his back toward her, surrendering to her domination. Her lips moved from his mouth to his neck and back again while she unbuttoned his shirt and undid his pants. Her hand slid down between his legs caressing his hardness.

Faster than he could have imagined, her dress came off and her exquisite bare breasts rubbed against his chest while her aggressive kisses covered him ending with her hot wet tongue darting in and out of his ear punctuated by whispers of, "Mon chéri." She pushed him down on a table and mounted him with a few hard thrusts that sent him into paroxysms of ecstasy, then she laid there for some time with her head on his chest caressing his face and hair.

To Maury's surprise and delight, a chauffeur driven limousine waited for him when he left the lab later that afternoon that whisked him off to a lavish penthouse where everything seemed to be made of white marble and gold, including the frames on the richly detailed paintings on the walls. Luxurious overstuffed white chairs and couches sat on a large plush white carpet in front of a floor to ceiling circular glass wall that provided a stunning view of San Diego sprawled out below them. The city's twinkling lights added to the magic of it all.

Margaux stood at the center of the room, a vision of beauty in a sheer silk low cut teal mini dress that barely covered her creamy thighs. A sumptuous candlelit feast behind her spread out on a long mahogany table in front of a candlelit sparkling window arranged with silver ice filled buckets of champagne, shrimp, crab's legs, strawberries, and other fruits alongside gold platters heaped with beef, turkey, and ham.

"I guess this means you are interested in investing," Maury said, struggling not to show his amazement.

Margaux giggled. "Of course, mon chéri. It's all arranged with papa. Please, sit. You must be ravenous after all your hard work today."

He took a seat across from her and she snapped her fingers. A sexy maid in a dark outfit and a frilly white apron served him and attended to his every need while Margaux's adoring gaze stayed on him as if he were the only thing in the room. His plate was whisked away the moment he finished.

Looking up, he saw that Margaux had barely eaten and her attention hadn't faltered making him feel self-conscious. She smiled dreamily, clapped her hands, and the maid disappeared, then she rose from her chair and let her dress slip to the floor revealing her perfect figure.

She floated toward him, pushed his chair back, took off his shoes, undid his pants, and pulled them off, then she put a fresh strawberry in her mouth and sat on his lap pressing her lips to his, easing it into his mouth while sliding down on him, repeating the afternoon's performance.

They made love twice more that night and cuddled for some time in her massive lace draped four poster canopy bed before Maury drifted off, waking in the predawn hours to the gentle sound of her breathing beside him. Not wanting to wake her, he slipped out the door and called an Uber to take him to his lab where he showered and changed clothes.

Bleary-eyed and tapped out from his previous surreal pleasure filled afternoon and evening, beneath it all he sensed a glowing satisfaction at the thought that his long held dreams had come true.

It was still early to check phone and email messages, so he went to his lab to look in on Romeo and Juliet. He had rendered all the rats unconscious from his initial trials with chloroform and phenobarbital before cutting them open to examine them against controls. This was the first time he had let them live longer to observe long term outcomes.

He felt a muted sense of alarm when he found Romeo pinned to the corner of the terrarium by Juliet who arched her back while thrusting her buttocks against him. I gave her a big dose, he thought, which must have been massive in comparison to the one I gave Margaux. He made a mental note to recalculate an effective dosage by weight and smiled.

Love Potion Number Nine was a lot more powerful than he realized.

He went back to his office lost in thought, puzzling over the best way to calculate dosages when his cell phone rang. Thinking it might be an investor, he hit the Answer button. "Hello?"

"Where did you go, mon chéri?" Margaux said, sounding as if she were on the verge of tears. "I was so disappointed to find you gone. You do love me, don't you?"

"Of course I do, my love," he reassured her. "I had pressing duties to tend to and I was anxious to check up on Romeo and Juliet. I have some important follow through work to do with them."

Aah, Romeo and Juliet," she cooed. "That's who we are, no?" Her voice lifted, sounding like a little girl. "Can I come to your office to be with you?"

He sighed. "I would love that, my sweet," but I have some important meetings today with my staff and colleagues."

"Tonight? We can be together tonight?"

"Yes, my love, tonight."

"I cannot wait."

Maury felt like he was living in a fairy tale when he stepped into the waiting limousine, and in the nights that followed Margaux was in the back seat waiting for him in sexy lingerie where they had sex on the way to the penthouse followed by fancy dinners and still more sex. Leaving in the mornings became a growing challenge as Margaux clung to him, begging him to stay, but the limo remained at his disposal whenever he needed it.

He grew exhausted in a matter of days and he not only found it harder to concentrate at work, but he made a number of errors in the lab and he was falling behind in his work.

He awoke one morning to find Margaux literally clinging to him, begging him, "Please don't go, mon chéri. Stay."

"Darling, there is nothing I would like more," he said disentangling himself, but my timetable is slipping."

She drew back wide-eyed and pouting. "Don't you appreciate my love for you?"

"Of course I do!" He took her hand and caressed it. "You have to realize that this is the crowning achievement of my life's work."

She sat up straight in bed, a determined look hardening her features. "Then I will come with you."

"That would be wonderful," he said softly, "but not such a good idea."

She frowned.

"Your effervescent beauty would be a constant distraction." He kissed her hand. "It is hard enough as it is going through the day with your beautiful presence filling my thoughts. I would not get one thing done with you there."

Her expression softened, her eyelashes fluttered, and a dreamy smile washed over her face. "I understand," she said breathlessly.

Maury felt surprised at her unexpected surrender. He had expected more resistance.

He went into the lab with a new sense of purpose, hoping their relationship had taken a more balanced turn. As much as he reveled in all the sex, it had been moving from extreme pleasure into something bordering on pain.

He needed a rest.

The first thing he did when he arrived at the lab was to look in on his rats. To his dismay he found Romeo dead in the corner of the terrarium with Juliet on top of him thrusting her buttocks against his backside as if she were the male. He reached in behind her and snatched her up by the tail and dropped her twisting, turning, screeching, and trying to bite him when he dropped her into an empty terrarium where she ran around in circles, then he gently picked the limp Romeo up from the terrarium and readied him for an autopsy to discover his cause of death. Normally he would have done the autopsy himself, but he lacked motivation and he had a growing backlog of work to contend with which further dampened his mood, so he assigned the task to one of his trusted undergraduate assistants with instructions not to share her findings with anyone but him.

Aside from the setback of Romeo's passing, no investors had contacted him in the days since his demonstration and his highs of the past few days came crashing down around him, leaving him feeling downtrodden, hopeless, and heartbroken.

He went to his office and told Rebecca not to let anyone bother him unless it was a dire emergency, then he dropped down in front of his computer, reluctant to log in, and instead leaned back in his chair and dozed off.

His desk phone rang, startling him out of his slumber. Silently cursing Rebecca for disturbing him, he let it ring twice more to give him a moment to gather his thoughts, then he picked up.

"What is it?" he growled.

"I'm sorry to disturb you," she said.

"This better be good."

"More than good," she said in breathless excitement. "I just took a call from our bank. We just exceeded our investment goals by fifty percent."

"What?" His mind sparked to life and jump started his heartbeat. His throat went dry. "Say again."

"We just exceeded our investment goals by fifty percent."

"What? How? By who?"

She giggled. "Angelic Investors."

"Angelic Investors? I've never heard of them and I don't remember sending them a proposal or seeing anyone representing them at our demo."

Maury punched in his password and logged in to the Peptide Passions banking web site. Sure enough, fifteen million dollars had been deposited into their account from Angelic Investors LLC.

"Me neither," Rebecca said, jolting him from his stupor, "but it's an LLC, so my guess is that a group of investors must have formed it to stay diversified so no one of them took all the risks and all of them could share in any profits."

Maury's mind raced. "I want you to find out everything you can about them, but first I want you to call an immediate mandatory all hands staff meeting so we can share the news, then we'll follow up and find out who our angels are."

"Ten minutes in the conference room?"

"Perfect! Don't tell anyone what the meeting is about."

"Of course!"

Maury walked into the conference room which was buzzing with uncertainty. "Thank you all for coming." The room fell silent after he made his way to the front. "I have an important announcement to share that will radically change the direction of our company. I feel it is important to tell each and every one of you that we would not have come this far without your hard work and dedication and I love you all dearly."

"Here comes the axe," someone whispered.

Maury paused and looked down at the ground, drawing out the moment to the point of discomfort, then he looked up, smiling. "I'm happy to announce that we have exceeded our targeted startup financing goals."

The stunned silence felt palpable, then scattered gasps erupted into cheers and applause. In the midst of it the conference room door opened and Margaux glided into the room with her chauffer trailing behind her pushing a hand truck stacked with cases of Dom Perignon.

Maury felt anger at the way she had interrupted the meeting, followed by confusion when he realized that Margaux was the one behind Angelic Investors.

"Champagne for everyone!" She held up a bottle and then a second one. "And an additional bottle for you to take home to continue the celebration there."

More cheers and applause followed.

When the initial excitement calmed down, Maury took her gently by the arm. "We need to talk." He guided her back to his office while she sipped champagne and giggled.

He locked the door behind them. "I don't know what to say or where to start."

Margaux closed the blinds. "Right now, you don't need to say anything, mon chéri. We celebrate first with the language of love and we talk after."

"But…"

She silenced him with a kiss, pulled her dress up and sat facing him on his office chair for another round of passionate lovemaking. When they finished, he waited a few minutes until he couldn't contain his questions any longer. "I need to know…"

She put a finger to his lip and whispered in his ear, "Not yet," then she leaned back and spoke up. "I can't have you telling your employees that you love them all dearly. You love only me!"

He took her hand and kissed it, thinking how silly her sense of humor was for saying something so ludicrous. "Only you."

She smiled.

"Surely this investment has some conditions attached to it.

She caressed the side of his face. "The only caveat is that papa insists that I have an office here and a seat on the board of directors to oversee his investment."

"That sounds more than reasonable."

She giggled. "He also insists that you get the final say in all business matters."

Maury smiled. "Wow! That's not too hard to accept."

She nuzzled his neck.

"I'd also like to include a few more investors out of courtesy for their loyalty with the seed money they provided from the beginning," he said.

She stiffened. "No need. Papa has given you the exclusive."

Maury started to respond, but the finality in her voice and her body language told him that this was not the time for a disagreement, especially with so much on the line, so he checked himself and decided to follow up with the investors on his own.

"I'll have my staff set up an office for you with a phone, an email account, and access to the files you will need to keep track of the financials."

"I love you," she said nibbling on his ear.

The moment she left to plan a celebration dinner for them at Mr. A's, San Diego's premier penthouse restaurant with a spectacular view of San Diego, Maury emailed his seed investors with an invite to participate going forward as a thank you gesture for their loyalty. He signed the emails to his long standing female investors with an "XO", something his mother had always signed her notes to him with, and he signed the ones to the males with, "Yours in Love and Brotherhood."

After completing that task, Maury instructed his staff to set up an elegant office on the opposite corner of the building from him so Margaux could have everything she needed, while keeping her as far away from him as possible so she wouldn't be interrupting his work.

Maury surprised her that night at dinner when he told her he had arranged for her to get the most prized corner office location in the whole building, which pleased her, but she pouted when she discovered that it was at the opposite end of the building from him. After he explained to her how fitting and prestigious the corner location was, and to what lengths he went through to make it happen in minimal time she was appeased some, but still showed disappointment.

She moved into her new office a few days later.

When he didn't get any responses to the emails he sent to his seed investors, Maury had Rebecca check with his IT department to see if they had gone out. She called him back a few minutes later to report that Margaux had gone through every one of his emails and that a second set of emails had gone out after his from Margaux, who had cancelled all of the offers he had made, and ordered all the recipients to cease any contact with Peptide Passions or any of its employees.

Any questions or concerns were directed to a law firm that Maury had never heard of.

Incensed, he called his investors and was met with guarded responses or refusals to discuss the matter, mentioning their fear of lawsuits. The women sounded exceptionally frightened, and most of them did not want to talk about it, but after Maury's insistence, a few long time close friends and colleagues begged him not to say anything to Margaux, but she had called them with veiled threats of violence and warned to, "stay away from any contact with her man, or face unimaginable consequences."

Teeter-tottering between fear and rage, Maury had Rebecca check the company phone records as well as his cell phone records. To his dismay, she reported back to him that Margaux had also gone through every one of his phone records, which made him feel violated. When he looked through them he saw that all of the seed investors had been called, and the calls to the women were the longer calls.

This had all gone too far. He told Rebecca to hold all of his calls for the rest of the day and he stormed down the hall to the other side of the building to Margaux's office, only to find it empty.

He pulled out his cell phone and punched in her number with trembling fingers.

She picked up on the first ring. "Hello, mon chéri."

The sound of her voice sent a hurricane of emotions, chief among them rage conflicting with passion. Maury struggled for words, finally blurting, "We need to talk!"

"Yes, we do, mon chéri," she said dreamily. "I am waiting for you at the penthouse."

He hit the end button on his phone and left the building, only mildly surprised to find the limo waiting for him.

A smiling Margaux awaited him at the penthouse with a pitcher of martinis and two glasses already poured.

"We need to talk," he stammered, feeling his anger fuel an erection that he didn't want. "You had no right going through my emails and phone calls, and you had no right interfering with my business decisions, much less threatening and dismissing my seed investors."

Her smile disappeared, replaced by a wide-eyed grief stricken. expression. She dismissed her maids while tears welled up in her eyes, and in spite of his rage, Maury felt sorry for her and regretted his anger.

She handed him a drink with a trembling hand and he gulped it, trying to calm himself. He felt it hit him immediately, blunting his anger, but it still raged beneath the surface.

"*I* had no right," she sobbed, refilling his glass. Her eyes grew still wider. "*I* had no right," she repeated. "How could you ever sign your emails to those women with an X and an O meaning a kiss and a hug, "mon chéri? That is only for me, and me alone!"

Maury couldn't believe what he was hearing. "Darling," he pleaded. "That meant nothing! It is a term of affection that my mother signed her messages to me with, nothing more."

"A term of affection?" she cried out. "How could you use a term of affection with other women when your love is only for me? How can you tell your staff you love them when your love is only for me?"

"You don't undershtand," he slurred. "I don't love thoshe women like I love you, You are my one and only…"

The room tilted sideways and his vision blurred. Her hazy face, hardened and distorted by anger leaned in close to him. The last thing he saw was her fading grimace which frightened him as he plummeted into blackness.

He came to spread-eagled on her bed, his feet and wrists shackled, with her mounting him. Tears streamed down her face, while she babbled about the female investors she accused him of being unfaithful to her with.

"I cannot bear your roving eye any longer," she said, thrusting hard against him. She moved faster, writhing more with each thrust bringing him closer to a rapid climax until he reached the point of release. "If I can't have you to myself, then nobody else is going to have you either, Romeo my love."

To his shock and surprise she pulled out a long knife and cut his throat, following through by cutting hers. Her hot blood splashed over him, mingling with his while their bodies spasmed together in the mutual orgasm of their death throes.

The image of Juliet on top of Romeo thrusting her buttocks against his backside as if she were the male flooded his mind as his life ebbed from him like a receding tide, washing him out into oblivion, relief, and sweet release to the ocean of death that awaited him.

RAY BRADBURY VS THE ALIENS

Inspired by the imagination of Ray Bradbury's writings, the impact they had on me, and the impulse they instilled in me to be a writer, I made the pilgrimage to his childhood home in Waukegan Illinois. Aside from that long standing dream, something deeper that I could not fathom, more like feelings than words urged me there. My family thought it was a waste of time and money, but the desire to go called to me like a muffled voice from the depths of my being until it became an obsession to visit the magical place of Ray's childhood and immerse myself in all things Bradbury. I hoped that I could tap in to the core of his inspiration and channel that same infectious childlike wonder and energy that he embodied throughout his entire life.

I had stalled with an impenetrable case of writer's block and that little voice inside me convinced me that the only way I could break through it was to make the effort to go to what to me was a sacred place. To stay true to the spirit of it all I decided to make it a true pilgrimage and follow in Ray's footsteps, so I traveled by bus the same way he did in his early years and the closer I got to Waukegan the stronger my puzzling inner drive grew, making me feel like a salmon swimming upriver to spawn.

When the bus pulled up in downtown Waukegan, I stepped off into a warm summer day with idealistic visions of Green Town, **Something Wicked This Way Comes**, and **Dandelion Wine**. I had envisioned a charming rural burg with sun-dappled fields and pies cooling on windowsills, but what met me was the grim reality of a hollow semi-industrial corpse of a depressed town complete with homeless people lurking in the shade of an abandoned building with their shopping carts circled like an old west wagon train. My heart sank

159

at the sight of it, but this was *the* place and I had the now irrepressible urge to follow through.

The moment I stepped off the bus a scraggly, ragged Jesus look alike clutching a book that had to be a Bible from the way he reverently held it rose from the circle and stared at me as though he had been waiting. I returned his gaze for an uncomfortable moment while the bus doors hissed shut behind me and the bus roared off leaving me feeling exposed.

"Jesus", stood stock still, then his bedraggled flock all turned as one and gave me the same expectant stare. Butterflies in my stomach prompted me to move along. I had memorized a map of the town and planned to take a self-guided walking tour trying to envision how it looked back in Ray's enchanted childhood.

Still feeling self-conscious from the uninvited attention I headed for the Carnegie Library on 1 North Sheridan Road, which in some ways I thought of as more of Ray's home than the home itself. After all, it did contain the spark that eventually ignited into Ray's most famous work, Fahrenheit 451.

Built in 1903 after the town received $25,000 from Andrew Carnegie, self-taught Ray Bradbury spent much of his youth here. The library closed in the sixties and moved to a bigger location, but the old building still held a historic elegance evident in its wrought iron fence, turn-of-the-century faux pillars, stylized moldings and other ornamentation embellishing the top of the building and around its entryways and windows.

I closed my eyes and visualized young Ray hopping up the steps to the big double doors of its entrance and stood there immersing myself in the reverie until the back of my head tingled and the peculiar feeling of being watched filled me. I turned around, opening my eyes to see the sole figure of the statue-like homeless Jesus studying me from across the intersection.

I gave him a cautious nod, but got no acknowledgement, so I chalked it up to coincidence and my own sense of heebie-jeebies at the sorry state that Waukegan had fallen into, then I moved on. Still feeling like I was being watched, I kept looking behind me to see if I was being followed, but saw no one as I headed for Ray's boyhood home. After that I planned to go to Ray Bradbury Park to explore the ravine that lived so vividly in my imagination.

I found a charming grey squat house at 11 South St. James Street with newer siding, modern windows, and white trim topped at its center by a two-windowed second story dormer with a gabled roof. I imagined young Ray sitting up in that room reading comic books and letting his imagination run wild.

I looked up and down the empty street and didn't see a soul, not even Jesus, so I crossed my arms and leaned up against a telephone pole, then I closed my eyes and let my imagination play itself out in a movie in my mind's eye. I saw young Ray reading from a stack of comic books and saw toy dinosaurs and pictures of the solar system, Jules Verne, and Edgar Rice Burrows memorabilia on the walls of his room. I savored the imagery until the back of my head tingled again followed by the uneasy feeling of being watched. I looked behind me to see the homeless Jesus studying me from across the street holding his Bible to his chest.

Enough was enough. He might be a lost schizophrenic or something, but this was no coincidence and his congregation wasn't with him, so I didn't have to worry about dealing with more than one. It was time to ask him what he wanted. When I crossed the street to face him he stood still, waiting for me.

"Is there something I can do for you?" I said, expecting something like, *Have you accepted Jesus as your Lord and savior?*

What he said was, "Know the truth and it will set you free."

Pretty much the same thing as accepting Jesus, I thought. The tingling in my head increased, unleashing a wave of confusion and I couldn't think of what to say or how to respond to him.

He smiled and tapped his book. It wasn't a Bible. It was a catalog of some kind. "Don't worry, I mean you no harm," he continued. "I just want you to know that you will find the answers you seek on the next stop of your visit on the Dandelion Trail in Ray Bradbury Park, in that same enchanted place where Ray found much of his inspiration."

My mind broke loose as if a giant hand had let a bird fly free. "How the hell do you know?" I blurted, surprised at the way it came out. "How do you know where I'm going and why are you stalking me?"

His smile broadened and he pressed his book close to his chest with both hands, then he bowed and walked off. "See you there!"

"Hey, wait a minute…"

Jesus disappeared around the corner without a response.

I was a little spooked at how he affected me and I thought that he and his homeless congregation could be setting me up for a mugging down in the ravine, but in spite of the strange interaction I didn't feel any big threat, just my usual paranoid mental gymnastics undercut by that mysterious spawning urge. More than any trepidation I held, my curiosity drove me forward to the park, especially when his words replayed themselves in my head. *You will find the answers you seek on the next stop of your visit on the Dandelion Trail...*

I found Ray Bradbury Park at 99 North Park Avenue a pleasant place. Aside from colorful over the top playground equipment that seemed out of place I had the sense that I was visiting hallowed ground. I closed my eyes and envisioned Ray as a boy exploring its many wonders. It did feel different here, like I was being drawn and called by something bigger than me.

I opened my eyes when I felt the tingle again and spotted a commemorative brass plaque. I went to it and took a moment to pay homage to Ray, then I read a second plaque that explained his career with gaudy children's museum style graphics. Though seeming out of place, it was somehow appropriate. One of the things I loved the most about Ray was his lifetime childlike wonder.

The tingle grew, urging me forward and I moved on until I found the ravine behind the park. It struck me as a beautiful, evocative, slightly disturbing place and I could see how it must have stoked young Ray's imagination. I made my way down the ravine steps and felt a chill when I saw a smiling Jesus several yards downstream beside a fallen tree that crossed the water. He nodded and gestured me forward with his finger, then disappeared into a copse of oak trees by the side of the creek.

I hesitated and the tingle pulsed like an invisible hand pushing me forward. I moved slowly, listening to everything, but all I could hear was the soothing burble of the water, the calls of birds, and the sound of cars from somewhere off in the distance.

I went to the fallen tree and stopped again to listen. Hearing nothing more I looked toward the oaks and saw no movement. Against my better judgement, I crossed the stream on the fallen tree and eased through some low bushes before stepping into a small clearing, fully expecting to find a homeless camp.

My breath hitched when I saw what's called a large fairy ring, fairy circle, elf circle, elf ring, or pixie ring made up of the biggest mushrooms I had ever seen. Ray's story, "Boys! Raise Giant Mushrooms in Your Cellar!" flooded my mind.

My homeless Jesus was nowhere in sight, but his book sat dead center in the middle of the ring looking worn and battered and it had mushrooms growing out of its pages! After a moment of confusion I gingerly stepped into the ring, careful not to disturb anything. Leaning in closer I studied the barely legible title on the faded cover.

JOHNSON SMITH & CO. CATALOGUE

I reached down and the moment my hand touched it the birds stopped singing. All I could hear was the babbling of the water. The tingling in my head pulsed without sound making me feel like a metal detector finding its treasure. *Know the truth and it will set you free*, I thought, followed by, *What if I'm not ready for that?*

What sounded like an audible voice in my head, startled me when it said, *"Pick me!"*

I dropped the book and the biggest mushroom fell off beside it.

"Yes, that one. Pick it up and eat it."

The thought of eating it made my stomach clench.

"Know the truth and it will set you free."

My head tingled again followed by a maniacal urge to pick up the mushroom. After a brief struggle, curiosity won over fear and my urge turned into an obsession. My hand picked up the mushroom as if under its own volition, separate from my rational mind and the next thing I knew it was in my mouth and I was chewing. It felt spongy and had a bland earthy taste.

What was I doing? I stopped chewing and went to spit it out when the voice said, *"Don't! Finish!"* My jaw moved like the hand of a puppeteer controlled it and I swallowed.

The wind gusted, blowing the first few pages of the Johnson Smith Catalogue open to a large ad with a smiling kid that read:

BOYS! RAISE GIANT MUSHROOMS IN YOUR CELLAR!

In the next moment I felt outside of time and space where the normal rules of perception no longer applied. Colors with hues that defied description bombarded me, then blossomed in multicolored geometric progressions that could have been microcosmic quantum expressions, or unfolding galaxies. Words fall short in trying to articulate the full expansion I experienced. I can only approximate it when I say that I became the mushroom, the mushroom became me, then I became young Ray Bradbury, experiencing everything through his eyes, ears, and thoughts. *How wonderful,* I thought. *Possessed by the spirit of Ray Bradbury. What a blessing!*

I found myself living Ray's young life in fast forward, yet every detail was crystal clear, like part of my own strongest memories. I felt like I was both living in the middle of and watching the whole experience from outside of it like a movie unfolding inside of me on two levels.

As Ray, I lived and felt the thrill when the mailman came with the special delivery of "Abyssinian Amazon Mushrooms" from New Orleans and ran inside to the cellar to grow them. They grew unnaturally fast, pretty much overnight, and I had a powerful urge to eat one, but that only contributed to my uneasiness and the whole thing felt wrong in spite of the craving, then a voice in my head, jolted me when it said, *"Pick me!"*

The shock of it sent me running upstairs, thinking I was losing my mind until I overheard Mr. Fortnum, my friend Tom's dad talking to my dad outside the front door, telling him in a panicked voice that he was worried about the Earth being invaded by spores from a meteorite that crashed in the swamps near New Orleans. He said that the spores grew into mushrooms that someone ate, and alien spores took control of him. That person started a mushroom company and was distributing the spores to unsuspecting boys across the world, including Tom and me.

My dad didn't say anything to me that night, then Tom's mom called the next morning and said everything was fine and that Tom's dad was going on a business trip and taking her and Tom with him. When my dad asked about the strange behavior and the warning he had gotten, Tom's mom laughed and said that his dad was playing a practical joke.

I heard the terror in Mr. Fortnum's voice the night before, so this sudden change made things worse. I ran out the back door and ran the few block to Tom's house to ask him what was going on. When I got there I slowly went up the back steps and peeked into the kitchen before knocking. My heart stopped when I saw Tom and his parents at the kitchen table wolfing down mushroom sandwiches.

None of them spoke and all of them drooled as they chewed with a glazed faraway look in their eyes like docile cows chewing on cuds. I stepped away and backed down the steps to the cellar bulkhead. Easing open the unlocked storm door I moved into the darkness of the cellar where I found even bigger mushrooms than I had growing all over an overflowing table, onto the floor, and covering the walls.

The floor creaked above me and I heard the sound of chairs being pushed back from the table, so I hurried out of the cellar and through the backyard, running once again to the only place I thought I could find refuge and answers.

The library.

I spent most of the day there reading everything I could about mushrooms and discovered what I needed in a book on gardening that said vinegar worked as a natural fungicide and the acetic acid in it would kill mushrooms and hinder their return.

That night when the house was dark I crept into the kitchen and found my mom's white vinegar. Following the instructions from the library book I put on work gloves and covered my eyes with goggles, then I went down to the cellar and mixed four parts of water to one part vinegar and filled my mom's copper and brass garden bug sprayer.

By this time the mushrooms had more than doubled in size. My heart raced and I felt guilty like I was doing something terribly wrong and the closer I got to the mushrooms, the more this feeling grew. Battling the dueling urges to both eat one and run, I took a deep breath, and held the tip of the sprayer a few inches away from the mushrooms and sprayed them with a heavy dose of diluted vinegar.

They trembled and emitted high pitched nauseating squeals and confusion swept through me, but I continued pumping the sprayer and vomited when the last of the squeals faded to silence.

Fighting my terror, I trotted to Tom's house which was dark and empty. When I pulled up the cellar's bulkhead door, I heard a chorus of forlorn mewling that sounded like a bizarre mix of whining puppies and alley cats and felt an invisible force pushing me back.

Pushing through my fear, I repeated what I had done in my cellar and steeled myself as the unholy chorus of mournful cries tore through me, louder and more intense than the first time. When the last of the wails receded I felt depleted, like I had lost some part of me, then I dry heaved and staggered home where I fell into a deep, dreamless sleep.

Tom and his family never returned and a few short weeks later my dad made what seemed like an overnight decision to move to Los Angeles. As we left town my world became blurry and I found myself once again outside of time and space bombarded by colors with hues that defied description that filled me with multicolored geometric progressions.

I came to sitting on the ground in the middle of the fairy ring.

Drooling.

I looked up and saw homeless people surrounding me with their leader Jesus standing over me. None of them moved. They only stared, then I heard the voice of homeless Jesus speaking clearly in my head as if he spoke out loud, but his lips never moved.

Ray Bradbury defeated us here and a few others did the same across the country, but there was no way all of us could be found out. We're still taking over,

165

but not in the way you think. We are moving slow and steady, advancing our plan, but we decided that a different approach was in order. We discovered that we are far better served starting from the bottom up instead of the middle because no one will pay any attention to what they think they see as strange behavior. It's the perfect place to grow and expand our numbers without being found out. You are right in assuming that I am their leader.*

The colors and geometric patterns rushed in once again while he continued speaking in my mind.

My name is Tom Fortnum and I am possessed by the spirit of the aliens.

He smiled beatifically.

Now you are too.

Author's Note

Come into My Cellar by Ray Bradbury was originally published in **Galaxy Magazine** in October 1962, and was subsequently included in the short-story collection S is for Space.

The story is about an alien invasion in the form of fungi who take over the body and free will of whoever consumes them, and disperse by sending Special Delivery packages to new victims with mushrooms to be grown and eaten.

Ray mentioned having the idea for the story while eating steak and mushrooms with a group of editors, and not being taken seriously by them. He then joked that he didn't eat mushrooms for the following years.

The short story now titled **Special Delivery** written by Ray originally aired on Season 5 Episode 10 of Alfred Hitchcock Presents on November 29th 1959.

Boys! Raise Giant Mushrooms in Your Cellar aired thirty years later on Season 4: Episode 12 on The Ray Bradbury Theater on November 17, 1989

Some years ago I was honored when invited to write an essay for a limited edition tribute to Ray, which I titled ***A Ray of Light***.

A RAY OF LIGHT

In the early seventies I read a short story in a high school English class titled *There Will Come Soft Rains* that captured my imagination in a way that few stories could. Its opening burned an indelible image into my mind the same way the outlines of a family had been burned into the side of a computerized house where robots went through preprogrammed computerized chores in the aftermath of an atomic blast. This post apocalyptic family portrait created by Ray Bradbury still haunts me more than three decades after first reading it.

In the years that followed I discovered that I had a knack for writing, but never in my wildest imaginings did I think I would actually become a writer, and never in my even wilder imaginings could I conceive of knowing Ray Bradbury as a guiding light, an inspiration, and a loving, caring mentor.

In nineteen-eighty-eight I attended the Santa Barbara Writer's Conference for the first time, and on opening night I heard Ray kick off the conference with an outpouring of love, passion, and inspiration, not only for the written word, but for life in general.

"The hell with everything else", he exhorted. "Write for the love of it!"

Year after year I have returned to the conference, first as a student, then as a workshop leader, each time hearing this same message spoken in different ways with just as much passion, if not more, and each year my inspiration is rekindled anew.

In nineteen-ninety-four I published my first short story collection titled *The Small Dark Room of the Soul*. Friends and colleagues urged me to ask Ray for a blurb because we were affiliated through the conference, but I found myself in mortal terror at the thought of it.

Eventually I screwed up my courage and asked the advice of Sid Stebel, a friend, mentor, and a close friend of Ray's. Sid went to bat for me and eventually Ray blessed me with the words: "Bravo More!"

Never in my life had two simple words carried so much power.

Six years later when my first novel, *Land Without Evil* came out, I was once again urged to ask Ray for his blessing. During that time he suffered a major health setback that hospitalized him, so I gave up all hope of getting another blurb. To my amazement, soon after my request I received a typed yellow card signed by Ray, full of encouragement, apologizing for not getting back to me sooner, saying he couldn't read my work, but giving me permission to use his original blurb. I treasure that card and have it framed and displayed prominently in my writing space beside a picture of Ray and me. I consider myself blessed to know him personally and doubly blessed by the wish he granted me.

Cinderella had her fairy godmother to inspire her with loving light beyond her wildest imaginings, and I have my own Ray of light, a writing godfather who did the same for me.

ABOUT THE AUTHOR

Matthew J. Pallamary's works have been translated into Spanish, Portuguese, Italian, Norwegian, French, and German. His historical novel of first contact between shamans and Jesuits in 18th century South America, titled, *Land Without Evil* received rave reviews along with a San Diego Book Award for mainstream fiction. It was also adapted into a full-length stage and sky show, co-written with and directed by Agent Red and performed by Sky Candy, an Austin Texas aerial group. The making of the show was the subject of a PBS series, Arts in Context episode, which garnered an EMMY nomination.

His nonfiction book, *The Infinity Zone: A Transcendent Approach to Peak Performance* is a collaboration with professional tennis coach Paul Mayberry that offers a fascinating exploration of the phenomenon that occurs at the nexus of perfect form and motion. *The Infinity Zone* took 1ˢᵗ place in the International Book Awards, New Age category and was a finalist in the San Diego Book Awards.

His first book, a short story collection titled *The Small Dark Room Of The Soul* was mentioned in The Year's Best Horror and Fantasy and received praise from Ray Bradbury and has been released as an audio book.

His second collection, *A Short Walk to the Other Side* was an Award Winning Finalist in the International Book Awards, an Award Winning Finalist in the USA Best Book Awards, and an Award Winning Finalist in the San Diego Book Awards. It has been released as an audio book.

DreamLand a novel about computer generated dreaming, written with legendary DJ Ken Reeth won first place in the Independent e-Book Award in the Horror/Thriller category and was an Award Winning Finalist in the San Diego Book Awards. It has also been released as an audio book.

It's sequel, ***n0thing*** is titled after the main character, who in the real world is his nephew, an international Counter-Strike gaming champion. After winning what amounts to the Super Bowl of gaming, n0thing and his winning teammates, are recruited as a literal "dream team" whose mission is to go into the nightmares of battle scarred veterans and rescue them from their traumatic memories while becoming ambassadors for a gaming platform that exceeds virtual reality with an experience that pushes the boundaries of reality itself.

Eye of the Predator was an Award Winning Finalist in the Visionary Fiction category of the International Book Awards. ***Eye of the Predator*** is a supernatural thriller about a zoologist who discovers that he can go into the minds of animals.

CyberChrist was an Award Winning Finalist in the Thriller/Adventure category of the International Book Awards. ***CyberChrist*** is the story of a prize winning journalist who receives an email from a man who claims to have discovered immortality by turning off the aging gene in a 15 year old boy with an aging disorder. The forwarded email becomes the basis for an online church built around the boy, calling him CyberChrist. It has also been released as an audio book.

Phantastic Fiction – A Shamanic Approach to Story took first place in the International Book Awards Writing/Publishing category. ***Phantastic Fiction*** is Matt's guide to dramatic writing that grew out of his popular Phantastic Fiction Workshop.

Night Whispers was an Award Winning Finalist in the Horror category of the International Book Awards. Set in the Boston neighborhood of Dorchester, ***Night Whispers*** is the story of Nick Powers, who loses consciousness after crashing in a stolen car and comes to hearing whispering voices in his mind. When he sees a homeless man arguing with himself, Nick realizes that the whispers in his head are the other side of the argument.

His memoir ***Spirit Matters*** detailing his journeys to Peru, working with shamanic plant medicines took first place in the San Diego Book Awards Spiritual Book Category, and was an Award-Winning Finalist in the autobiography/memoir category of the National Best Book

Awards.

The Center Of The Universe Is Right Between Your Eyes But Home Is Where The Heart Is was an Award Winning Finalist in the International Book Awards. Based on a lifetime of research into shamanism, visionary states, the evolution of written communication and the roots of storytelling, award-winning author, editor, and shamanic explorer Matthew J. Pallamary takes those with open minds courageous enough to question the illusions that most of us think of as real on an expansive journey that pierces the veil of reality itself.

AfterLife: The Adventures of a Lost Soul was inspired by real life events, William Peter Blatty's *The Exorcist,* and the dynamics of demonic possession.

Matt has also produced and directed *The Santa Barbara Writers Conference Scrapbook* documentary film and co-wrote the book of the same title in collaboration with Y. Armando Nieto, and conference founder Mary Conrad.

Death: (A Love Story) a first person narrative spoken by the omniscient voice of Death itself, who says, "I'm here to tell you stories and share some science, history, and myths, all of which are your creations that I want to share to help you understand me more. You have seen me as Satan, Anubis, Mot, Thanatos, God, the Devil, loving, punitive, dark, light – the list goes on and on! It is my sincerest hope that our friendly reintroduction here will change the way you think of me, and maybe in some small way reflect the depth of the love I have for you.

Picaflor is the sequel to *Spirit Matters*, a San Diego Book Award winner and an Award-Winning Finalist in the National Best Book Awards that chronicles the two decades since of Matthew (Mateo) J. Pallamary's adventures in *Spirit Matters* through the mountains, deserts, and jungles of North, Central, and South America pursuing his studies of shamanism and visionary experience working with plant medicines and shamanic plant diets, among them Ayahuasca, Peyote, San Pedro cactus, and many more.

Picaflores: The Nerve Endings of GOD was an Award Winning Finalist in the International Book Awards that details a magical, otherworldly, intimate connection with the spirit of hummingbirds that comes from two decades of visionary journeys experienced within the context of shamanic plant diets in the Peruvian Amazon. It also contains a treasure trove of pre-Columbian myths about hummingbirds and an in-depth collection of amazing facts and figures about these magical creatures.

Holographicosmic Man: The Holographic Heart of the Golden Mean is an amalgam of quantum physics, mathematics, geometry, ancient texts, current research, ancient architecture, beliefs, and myths, astronomy, anthropology, human anatomy, brain structure, shamanism, neuroscience, neuropsychology, indigenous wisdom, astrophysics, neurophysiology, holography, neuroanatomy, neurocardiology, cosmometry, cosmology, biology, and more.

Matt's work has appeared in Oui, New Dimensions, The Iconoclast, Starbright, Infinity, Passport, The Short Story Digest, Redcat, The San Diego Writer's Monthly, Connotations, Phantasm, Essentially You, The Haven Journal, The Hurricanes & Swan Songs Anthology, The Santa Barbara Literary Journal, The Closed Eye Open, The Montecito Journal, and many others. His fiction has been featured in The San Diego Union Tribune which he has also reviewed books for, and his work has been heard on KPBS-FM in San Diego, KUCI FM in Irvine, television Channel Three in Santa Barbara, and The Susan Cameron Block Show in Vancouver. He has been a guest on the following nationally syndicated talk shows; Coast to Coast with George Noory, Paul Rodriguez, In The Light with Michelle Whitedove, Susun Weed, Medicine Woman, Inner Journey with Greg Friedman, Night Dreams, and Environmental Directions Radio series. Matt has appeared on the following television shows; Bridging Heaven and Earth, Elyssa's Raw and Wild Food Show, Things That Matter, Literary Gumbo, Indie Authors TV, Spiritually Raw, and ECONEWS. He has also been a frequent guest on numerous podcasts, among them, The Psychedelic Salon, Black Light in the Attic, Third Eye Drops, C-Realm, Psychedelics Today, Voices in the Dark, Adventures Through the Mind, Beyond the Veil, Mind Escape, and many others.

Matt received the Man of the Year Award from San Diego Writer's Monthly Magazine and has taught a fiction workshop at the **Southern California Writers' Conference** in San Diego, Palm Springs, and Los Angeles, and at the **Santa Barbara Writers' Conference** for over thirty years. He has lectured at the Greater Los Angeles Writer's Conference, the Getting It Write conference in Oregon, the Saddleback Writers' Conference, the Rio Grande Writers' Seminar, the National Council of Teachers of English, The San Diego Writer's and Editor's Guild, The San Diego Book Publicists, The Pacific Institute for Professional Writing, The 805 Writers Conference, The College of Central Florida, Yakima Valley College in Washington, The Yakima Public School System, and he has been a panelist at the World Fantasy

Convention, Con-Dor, and Coppercon. He is presently Editor in Chief of Mystic Ink Publishing.

Matt was a featured lecturer and performer at the **Mysteries of the Amazon** exhibit at the Appleton Museum in Ocala Florida and The Larson Gallery in Yakima Washington. He frequently visits the mountains, deserts, and jungles of North, Central, and South America pursuing his studies of shamanism.

MATTPALLAMARY.COM

BOOKS BY MATTHEW J. PALLAMARY

THE SMALL DARK ROOM OF THE SOUL

LAND WITHOUT EVIL

SPIRIT MATTERS

DREAMLAND (WITH KEN REETH)

THE INFINITY ZONE (WITH PAUL MAYBERRY)

A SHORT WALK TO THE OTHER SIDE

CYBERCHRIST

EYE OF THE PREDATOR

PHANTASTIC FICTION

NIGHT WHISPERS

THE SANTA BARABARA WRITERS CONFERENCE SCRAPBOOK
(WITH MARY CONRAD & Y. ARMANDO NIETO)

n0THING

AFTERLIFE: THE ADVENTURES OF A LOST SOUL

THE CENTER OF THE UNIVERSE IS RIGHT BETWEEN
YOUR EYES BUT HOME IS WHERE THE HEART IS

DEATH: (A LOVE STORY)

PICAFLOR

PICAFLORES: THE NERVE ENDINGS OF GOD

HOLOGRAPHICOSMIC MAN

www.ingramcontent.com/pod-product-compliance
Lightning Source LLC
Chambersburg PA
CBHW060115260626
47160CB00005B/1900